Still Here

Coleen Muller

Contents

All Over This Small Town

O ctober 2013

Susanna's POV

Brushing my long auburn hair off my face with the back of my arm I focused on icing the cookies for the local DAR tea that Mary Vines called in last minute after her oven went out. Being up since four this morning to get just the daily orders baked, I was running on fumes with it barely being early afternoon. I heard the bells jingle over the front door along with praying that Cheyenne would take care of whomever it was giving me the time to get this done.

It was at least Friday. My cousin Stephanie opened the bakery for me on Saturdays letting me have a full day off since I usually used Sunday evenings to prep for the week. I had been told more than once to hire someone else to help out. Making sure the icing on the flag shaped cookies formed the way I wanted, I bit my lip against a snort hearing Cheyenne flirting with the customer out front. Josh, my other day time helper walked into the back grabbing another tray of pumpkin shaped cookies rolling his eyes behind dark framed glasses.

"She at it again?" I asked with a snicker making him sigh. Poor kid was in his third year of college and half in love with the buxom blonde that worked for me. He hung his head nodding making the shaggy blonde locks drape into his eyes. I gave him a soft smile. "Josh, honey I have told you that you can do better than her. I've known Cheyenne a long time. She has always been a flirt. Plus already reminded you she is older than you."

"I know," he grumbled. I was about to say more when a loud voice cut through the bakery.

"Ohhhhhh Suzie Q!!!" they drawled just adding to their Georgia twang. I couldn't help but smile as I wiped my hands on the apron I was wearing. Pretty sure there was flour somewhere on my face or in my hair. Always was. Josh followed me out heading to the load display case arranging the cookies. Cheyenne was handling the coffee order of Mr. Johnson who came by for a cup every afternoon. I walked over to the low end of the counter seeing the grinning idiot facing me. I got a wide smile. "Ahh there she is. I need two dozen chocolate cupcakes sweetheart."

"And if I don't have any," I teased biting my bottom lip seeing his face fall. I reached out pushing down the top of his blonde mohawk earning me a glare before batting my hands away. I laughed shaking my head. "I always keep them in stock just in case. But only for you Bennie Boo. You are the one who claims you can't live without them."

"Swear Suzie Q," Ben chuckled crossing his tattooed arms over his chest with a smirk. "If you weren't out of my league I would marry you just for your baking skills."

"Then you would weigh five hundred pounds and I'd never get out of the kitchen," I sassed back putting a hand on my hip shaking a finger at him. "You have the biggest sweet tooth in all of north Georgia I do believe."

"Could be that I am just sweet on you," he teased bracing his big hands on the counter while I reached for a box to fill his order. I hip checked Josh out of the way and bit back a groan at Cheyenne throwing her shoulders back pushing her boobs up hoping Ben would notice. Swear she did this anytime he came in. I let out a snort putting cupcakes in the box. Wasn't unusual for him to come by for a bigger order when getting on the road.

"On the road this weekend?" I asked busying myself with my task smiling at a couple other regulars coming in. Ben shook his head shoving his hands into the pocket of his ripped jeans.

"Nah," he said with grin. "Done for a few weeks. Been in the studio. What you got going on tonight Suz?"

"Wine and my pajamas," I said with a heavenly sigh closing my eyes. "May watch the food network." Cheyenne scoffed rolling her eyes. Oh I knew she would be on the prowl for her weekend dick since she struck out with Ben yet again. "What can I say, hit my late twenties and I like to live dangerously."

"Aw that's cute that you think you get to stay in tonight," Ben teased with a wicked gleam to his eyes. A look that I had been seeing since high school. "Getting lucky it's going to be cool tonight. Bonfire and you aren't missing it."

"No Ben," I whined stomping my foot. He passed the money for the cupcakes over to Josh before tugging it out of my hands with a smirk blowing a kiss at me. "I mean it no!"

"Not the acceptable answer Suzie Q," he said with a shrug backing to the door. "You either show up or I drag you out of the house. You're not old nor are you dead yet! Better show your ass later or I will send Tiffany after you."

"Shit," I sighed hearing the bells jingle as Ben walked out. His cousin was hell on wheels and had been my best friend since high school. There was no getting out of going to this bonfire wherever it was even if I wanted to.

A few hours later a hard pounding on my front door made me groan. I sat the mascara wand down as I heard the door slam followed by footsteps a second later. A grinning blonde walked into my bathroom hip checking me away from the mirror before brandishing a tube of red lipstick. I narrowed my amber colored eyes at her as Tiffany grinned at me.

"Oh stop pouting Suz," she snickered pursing her lips passing me the lipstick. I rolled my eyes shaking my head smothering a yawn. "You need a night out. Been a while since all you do is bury yourself in work."

"Burying myself in work as you say is running my business Tiff," I sighed glaring at her. All I really wanted to do was curl up to go to bed early. I poked my lip out making her laugh as she fluffed the curled ends of my hair. "Please don't make me go."

"It's cute when you beg," Tiffany chuckled tapping my chin with a hot pink nail before giving my outfit a once over. "I'm digging the tight jeans. But that hoodie has got to go. Come on let me dig you out something."

"Tifffff...." I whined stomping my foot to no avail as she drug me to my closet. I growled at her being totally ignored. "Fine! But better make sure my boobs are covered!"

Brantley's POV

I tamped down a sigh watching the crowd around the bonfire. Ben was flirting with some girl that I prayed for his sake was over twenty-one. If she was out here with this group she better be. I wasn't going to come until Ben and Kolby talked me into it. I only had a few weeks of down time before another leg of touring and I needed to finish up a song I was working on for the new album. It had been a busy year that still hadn't wound down yet. Go from the beginning of the year to planning to get married and then now single and free as a bird. I planned on staying that way. I was too busy from anyone steady anyhow.

"Quit moping bro and find a woman," Kolby said from beside me turning up his beer then shooting me a smirk as I flipped him off. "What? You have been a little grouchy lately."

"Fuck off," I grumbled running a hand over my backwards hat kicking my leg against his from the back of my tailgate. I smirked at him. "We both know finding a woman is the easy part."

"Getting cocky in our old age are we," my not so little brother sassed back. I grinned ruffling the top of his head turning his hat sideways. A blonde shot both of us a flirty grin from the next truck over making Kolby sit up straight puffing his chest out. I was about to shove Kolby her direction with a flash of tumbled dark auburn hair caught the corner of my eye. My damn brother saw the redhead same time I did letting out a low whistle. "Holy....helllllllllll look at them jeans."

"Dayummm...." I murmured appreciatively. There was something familiar about her, but I couldn't put my finger on it. Then I saw Ben pick her up swinging her around in a hug and studied the blonde next to her in a leather jacket making recognition click. I felt my jaw drop a little. No way in hell. "Holy fuck."

"Knew that woman was hiding sex appeal behind her aprons," Kolby murmured giving me a wink then reaching over to close my mouth before he started laughing. "Did you just finally figure out who she is? Hell B, Ben gets two dozen of her cupcakes her time y'all get on the road. Wait a minute.....you didn't know. Thought you had a little bit of a crush on her in high school. Even though she was like what a freshman your senior year?"

"Yea," I murmured watching her throw her head back laughing at something Tiffany said. Now Tiff, I saw a good bit because she always tried to
make a show when we were close. Her and Ben were really close. All these
years I never thought to ask her about her best friend to find out what
happened with her. If I was honest, I didn't think much about it then
with all that was going on in my life. I remembered the shy little redhead
had always been quiet. God bless at the woman she had grown into. I sat
my bottle of water down on the tailgate about to hope down when Kolby
stood up stretching his arms over his head adjusting his hat. I narrowed
my eyes at him as he turned around grinning at me. "Where the hell you
going?"

"I'm going to find out what the cupcake specials are for next week," he said
with an evil smile. I growled at my little brother debating on tackling him
to the ground knocking his ass out but stopped knowing Mama would
beat my ass if he showed up to church Sunday morning with a black eye.
He would tattle on me in a heartbeat. I shrugged deciding an ear tug was
worth it. I jumped down catching my long legged brother mid-stride and
factored how much beer he had drank into hooking my foot on the back of
his calf sending him face planting into the dirt. He yelped when he landed
as I started laughing. Kolby rolled over holding his chin as he glared up at
me. "What the hell B!"

"Dang Ko," I chuckled taunting him with a grin as he flipped me off.
"Guess you should slow down on the beer. I'll be sure to find out what
those specials are for ya little brother. Besides I'm calling dibs."

"You can't call dibs on a woman!" he called after me as I strutted towards
Ben. "Not like you do Mama's fried chicken!"

"Snooze you lose little brother!" I said waving at him as I walked over seeing
Ben passing a couple red cups to the girls laughing at something Tiffany
was teasing him about. A pair of amber colored eyes lifted as I approached

widening. I could swear I saw a blush tease across Susanna's cheeks as I winked at her before throwing my arm around Ben's shoulders. I gave both girls a flirty smile. "Bennie Boo what are you doing man?"

"Dammit BG," Ben sighed rolling his eyes as Tiffany cracking up laughing and a quiet giggle slipped past Susanna's lips. Drove him nuts to be called that and I knew it. "You remember my cousin Tiffany, and this is her best friend Susanna. Makes the best cupcakes this side of the Mississippi man."

"So I have heard," I said turning my attention to Susanna smacking my lips together after running my tongue over my bottom lip. Tiffany smothered a laugh behind her cup as Susanna froze in place. " Mmmmm.....and have tasted since Ben here always gets us some for the road. I remember you from high school darlin. Though it has been a while."

"Yea it has," Susanna choked out after Tiffany elbowed her making me bite back a smile. She was shy. I see that hadn't changed over the years. I was about to step a little closer to Susanna when a hand grabbed my arm. I turned my head with the beginning of a growl but stopped seeing Eli standing there giving me a look.

"Need your help for a second BG," he said with an amused grin on his lips. I was about to cold cock him because I was betting it was a bullshit reason and he was going to give me hell for attempting to flirt with Susanna. Even after all these years he still loved to bust my balls. I turned looking back at Susanna as Eli drug me off.

"I'll be back to find you later darlin," I called out making her blush with a wink and a smile. Hmm..wonder if more than her cheeks blushed. I would have to find out.

As The Hymn Book Flies

Susanna's POV

"Jesus that smirk is gonna kill me," I murmured under my breath sitting on a log near the fire. I squeezed my thighs together praying it was the tequila shots that Tiffany and Ben had been giving me as I felt the liquor swirl through my veins. Not the looks and smiles I kept getting. It was the booze. Just the booze. Tiffany let out a snort shaking her head. I guess I wasn't as quiet as I would have liked. I closed my eyes in mortification. "I didn't whisper that did I?"

"Nope," Tiffany said with a snicker leaning against me. I laid my head on her shoulder feeling a pair of eyes searching for mine across the fire. That man was being a flirt that was all it was. Nothing more. Tiff leaned down to whisper in my ear. "Someone keeps watching you. I'd go for it Suz. You always had a crush on him in high school."

"The man just ended things with his fiancée a few months ago," I grumbled realizing my words were starting to slur. "I'm not even in his league anyhow."

"Oh whatever," she said slapping my hand. "His eyes have followed you since Eli drug him away." The sound of a guitar being strummed pulled both of our attention as Brantley shot me a wink before he started to sing. Ben grabbed a bucket he found somewhere to tap along to the beat. Eyes stayed locked on mine the entire time Brantley was singing "Dust on The Bottle". Lord help me that man had a sinful voice.

The next morning, I stumbled out of my bedroom blindly in search of the coffee pot and in desperate need of some aspirin. I held my aching head with one hand wincing at the bright sunlight spilling in. My phone had been dead on my nightstand. Between lack of sleep and the tequila last night I was hurting. The smell of coffee made my feet skid to a stop on the cold tile floor of my kitchen. I didn't remember setting the timer before Tiffany and I left last night. Trying to force my bleary eyes to adjust, I expected to see my best friend lounging in my kitchen.

Instead, I was greeted with a tattooed man giving me a sleepy smile. I yelped trying to back pedal out of the kitchen only to trip over my feet. Closing my eyes against the impending collision with the floor, I braced for impact. But it never came as a pair of warm hands gripped my waist yanking me back up. Bracing my hands on Brantley's bare chest, I tried to gather myself. Realizing where my hands where, I quickly pulled them away stepping back.

"What are you doing here?" I croaked out. He passed me a steaming mug of coffee with a chuckle.

"You were pretty hammered last night darlin," he told me softly. "So was Tiffany. Ben got her home and I told him I would make sure you did. I slept on the couch in case you needed anything."

"Oh," I murmured lowly in deference to my raging hangover feeling the first sips of caffeine fire through my system that had nothing to do with the man standing in front of me in just a low slung pair of sweatpants. It was then that I noticed the black t-shirt I was wearing that I knew wasn't mine. I became aware of the fact that it brushed the tops of my thighs leaving me in nothing more than it and my black lace under wear. My head jerked up meeting Brantley's eyes realizing he was staring at my legs. Snaking a hand out, I smacked his chest causing him to jump back in surprise. "What the hell happened last night?" Why am I in your shirt?"

"Because you spilled your last drink all down yours," Brantley said stretching the arm not holding coffee over his head making those pants slip a little more. Damn, that v-line I could trace with my tongue and keep going. Fingers snapping made my eyes jerk up to meet a laughing pair of green ones. "My eyes are up here Susie Q." I glared up at him as he chuckled making my traitorous nipples pebble at the sound.

"Tiffany was sober enough to help you get changed last night but couldn't find your pajamas. Claimed my shirt would do. I didn't see a thing sweetheart even though you did purposely flash me on the ride here. I almost ran off the road at that sweet, sweet, sight. Black lace is a good look against your skin."

"Kill me now," I moaned in mortification. "So, you really did crash on the couch?"

"Yes mam," Brantley answered with a grin reaching for me. "It was surprisingly comfortable. Would have been more comfortable snuggled up to you though."

Realizing the situation I was in, I back pedaled out of my kitchen shaking my head. I held a hand up as Brantley stepped closer to me.

"Don't," I hissed shaking my finger at him as his eyes widened. "You realize that we will be the talk of the supposed church prayer chain!"

"No we won't," Brantley scoffed rolling his eyes. "They have better things to worry about. "Then what I meant hit him. What does he do, he bursts out laughing the ass. He gave me a wink. "Worried about having that good girl reputation tarnished by possibly the preacher seeing my truck in your driveway. Wait, doesn't Ms. Cain, our high school algebra teacher live just down the street?"

"You may think this is funny," I snarled stomping my bare foot. "But I do have a business to run here."

"Well come here baby girl," Brantley murmured trying to wrap his arms around me. Lord help me the temptation was there. Something I had dreamed about ten years ago. "We can make good on what will be said anyhow."

A low whimper slipped past my lips seeing his head lower to mine. But good sense won out over my hormones. I braced both my palms against his warm chest shoving him back then pointed at my front door.

"Get out!" I growled taking him by surprise. Well tough shit if he didn't want to hear no. I turned on my heel stalking towards my bedroom. "I mean it Brantley!"

Sunday morning I hurried into church late after oversleeping. I had been up half the night stress baking. At least it meant a jump start on my prep for the week. There was a complicated wedding cake that was going to give me fits. I ducked in the side door keeping my head down feeling like the eyes of the whole town were on me. I slid into the pew beside Mama. Her green eyes glittering with questions as she raised an eyebrow at me. I ignored the look leaning down to put my purse at my feet, crossing my legs then sitting back up to grab the bulletin Daddy passed me. I pretended to be really interested in it. I smothered a groan when Mama's hand landed on my arm.

"Baby," she murmured pulling my attention to her as she leaned closer. "What's this I hear about you finally taking the time for a date?" I could practically hear the silent squeal in her voice. "Why didn't you call and tell me?"

"Mama," I said through clenched teeth. Tiffany turned around with a grin as I glared at her. I almost yanked the end of her blonde curls right there. "It wasn't like that."

"Then why was Brantley at your house honey?" she asked with wide eyes. I heard Daddy clear his throat no doubt wishing he was home cleaning his gun. I sighed shaking my head. " I mean it is perfectly okay if you as you kids say got some. Been a little grouchy lately. What? You had a huge crush on him in high school. I remember those papers signed Mrs....."

"Mama," I hissed turning red. "Would you hush. Want the truth? I had a little too much at the bonfire the other night because a certain blonde in front of us kept supplying me. BG was nice enough to give me a ride home and make sure I was okay. That is all. Nothing happened and nothing is gonna happen Mama."

I heard Tiffany let out a snort in front of me and I felt a hand pop the back of my shoulder. I turned my head meeting Daddy's brown eyes with a sheepish smile. He sooo reached behind Mama and popped me. He gave me a wry grin leaning around Mama squeezing my knee.

"Ladies," he chuckled. "Y'all behave please. And Susie Q, bring your new beau by to meet us soon."

"Really Daddy," I sighed rolling my eyes. "What is this the 1950's? It's not even like that, plus you coached Brantley and Kolby both in baseball. You know him. Can we drop this?"

"Well then I hope you are saying extra prayers sweetheart," Mama sighed patting my hand. "Don't want to be known as the town hussy."

I was about to argue back with her when the choir started singing. I stood up singing along from my hymnal mentally plotting to get Tiffany back for this weekend the first chance I got. The preacher called from us to be seated starting the sermon. He looked around the room with a quiet chuckle.

"Today we are going to talk about the sanctity of marriage," he said in his smooth baritone that Georgia drawl so evident. He gave a wink. "While I get it's not that hip to most young folk today, well y'all could be a little more discreet."

Right then and there I felt like the sermon was directed at me. I felt myself blush from the top of my head to the tip of my toes. A cough had my head turning to the left glancing across the aisle. Brantley was sitting with his mama between him in Kolby. He had his hand lifted covering his mouth as his shoulders shook in silent laughter. Kolby was red faced from keeping a laugh in. I glanced back to Tiffany whose shoulders were shaking as a snort bubbled out.

My fingers tightened around the hymnal still in my hand as Brantley turned his head locking his eyes with mine. Then he had the nerve to wink at me. I was in the process of raising the hymnal with the intention of throwing it at him when Mama thumped the back of my head making me drop it. As I bent over to retrieve it I took satisfaction in sweet Ms. Becky smacking both her sons with the bulletin shushing them.

By the time the service was over I had never been so glad to get out of there in my life. I hugged Mama and kissed Daddy telling them I would call them later. I was missing out on Sunday dinner to work on filling an order that had to be done for tomorrow. Digging my keys out of my purse, I let out a squeak when I collided with a solid chest. Cologne with just a touch of cigarette smoke teased my nose.

"Careful darlin," Brantley said softly making me take a step back. A big hand snaked out wrapping around my arm making my stomach swirl with butterflies. The senior ladies bible study group walked by heading to their cars and Mable Jenkins almost tripped over her feet seeing us together. I could hear their shushed whispers with someone looking back over their shoulder every couple of feet. Great, they all would be in the bakery this week asking questions. I tried to ignore how the black button up shirt molded to his chest as the hand on my arm slid up to cup my cheek. "Really? Gonna throw a hymnal at my head in the middle of church?"

"Well we were in God's house," I sassed putting my hands on my hips after batting his hand away. He glared back at me. "Was going to use what the good Lord gave me."

"Well now," Brantley said stepping closer to me leaning down brushing his lips against my ear that my French braid exposed. "I would love to see up close what he gave you."

My mouth dropped wide open at his words feeling my skin turn cherry red. The damn man made me so flustered it wasn't even funny. I turned on my heel stalking to my white Jeep just wanting to get out of there. Footsteps sounded behind me as I unlocked my door. It was opened before I got the chance making me turn around. Brantley held his hand out helping me climb in. Now the asshat wanted to play gentleman. Shit, he was just going to give them all more to talk about.

"I have to leave in the morning for Nashville," he said giving me a heart stopping smile. "But I would really like to take you to dinner when I get back. I won't take no for an answer."

Then before I could say anything he winked before walking off with his hands in his jeans pockets whistling "What A Friend We Have In Jesus".

Kolby's POV

I knew the moment my big brother cleared the doorway into Mama's kitchen because of the loud yelp followed by a string of cuss words that only got him a few more smacks. I jumped over the couch in my hurry to make it in there to see this. She had been lying in wait like a spider stalking her prey with that damnable wooden spoon handy. I propped my shoulder against the door frame of the kitchen watching them make circles around the table.

"Ouch Mama!" Brantley hollered as the spoon rapped across his knuckles colliding with his heavy biker rings. "What was that for?"

"I know you don't care son, but you have made that sweet girl be the talk of this town!" Mama huffed shaking her spoon at him with narrowed eyes. Brantley stopped standing straight up narrowing his own at her. Ohhhh...big bro was gonna get it. I had walked inside yesterday about the time she got the call that his truck had been spotted at Susanna's yesterday morning. I knew the truth and had tried to explain. Susanna had been drunk her and Tiffany both. B had been taking care of her. "If you can't keep it in your pants at least be discreet about it!"

"Mama!" Brantley snarled making her whack him again. "It wasn't like that honestly. Ask Kolby."

"Oh heck no B," I laughed holding my hands up. "Don't be dragging me into this."

"She had too much to drink the other night okay," he grumbled taking a few steps out of Mama's aim as she studied him. "Tiffany was her ride, but she wasn't much better off. Ben was in charge of her, so I offered to make sure that Susanna got home okay. She got sick on the way home, so I stayed to make sure she was okay. Nothing happened. I did ask her to dinner when I get back in town after church today."

"Listen to me Brantley Keith," Mama warned him shaking her finger. "And listen to me good. Susanna Hale is one of the sweetest girls you will ever meet. She has worked hard for what she has. Don't you go toying with her you hear me. You do and I will beat your tail black and blue son."

"Hear you loud and clear Mama," Brantley sighed looking over at me as I grinned. Oh, I knew he liked her more than he was letting on. Was funny to see that the auburn haired baker was keeping him on his toes. Not falling at his feet.

When A Scheme Comes Together

Sadie's POV

A long night waking up every couple of hours to check on Ryleigh's coughing had me needing an extra large cup of coffee to make it through my twelve hour shift. I can also use a sweet smile from the woman who makes the delicious nectar of the gods. Upon strolling into One Hale of a Bakery, my attention is drawn to the overly flustered Susanna that is usually calm and cheerful. She drums her fingers among the glass counter top grumbling over something that keeps her focused on her cell phone. Susanna jumps putting a hand to her chest when she notices my presence at the counter.

"Sadie, girl you startled me! The usual?" Susanna hurries off to the coffee bar behind her grabbing a medium cup before I can ask for an upgrade. I want to say something but her unusual behavior has me quietly keep to myself. She grabs a freshly cooked ham and cheese croissant from the rack behind her placing it next to my coffee on the counter. "Stupid email," She continues to mutter to herself over whatever has her worked up this morning. I slide over the cash arching a brow at the agitated woman.

"Email? Susanna, something has your feathers all ruffled up this morning. Everything okay?" She hands me back my change then props her elbows on the counter dropping her head into her hands.

"Just annoyed with being told I am doing something without letting me think about it," she sighs frustratedly never lifting her face. Then it clicks. Must be a man...or family.

"Ah, sounds like a man issue," my words pop Susanna's head out of her hands.

"No man. What are you talking about it? Man? Pfft." Susanna becomes more in a tizzy than before.

"Well," I say drawing out the accent that has grown on me, "if it's not a man, then why are your cheeks becoming a permanent shade of red?" I sip my coffee observing the auburn haired woman shake her head furiously. She stutters over trying to find the words to answer me while she sidesteps to rearrange the items in the display case. "Do you ever date? Maybe you need to relax a bit. You seem a tad stressed, hun."

"Excuse me?" Susanna jerks her head up from behind the glass case narrowing her eyes. I struck a nerve. Shit, she's the last person I want to make angry. There are certain people you don't piss off, that includes those who make your coffee. "I could say the same for you. We all would know if the new girl that moved here a couple years ago had a date." This is unlike Susanna. I've never heard her snap like this towards me or other customers. Maybe it's time for me to go.

"You're right, Susanna. I could use a date but I also don't live in a fairytale. Anyways, I should go. Hope you have a—," just before I could finish my sentence, the bells above the door jingle with a sound of heavy boots stomping in. Susanna's skin flushes once more seeing the figure behind me. Her eyes widen as she rounds the display case. She quickly makes her way to me as my eyes trail over the infamous bad boy of not only country music, but of Jackson County.

"Sorry about earlier. I, I.. uh I need to get back to work," Susanna smiles placing a hand on my arm guiding me towards the door.

"Why Susie Q are you trying to usher me out for some reason?" Giggling at Susanna, we both stop hearing snickering coming from the only other person in here who is studying Susanna like a restaurant menu. She drops her hand from my arm and stalks over to Brantley. I've never met him in person but between town gossip and my daughter's obsession for country music I felt that I knew his life story.

Excessive grumbling between the two occurs as soon as Susanna gets within inches of him. It becomes loud hushed whispers that is escalating into something more by the second. A big palm wraps around her waist yanking her close to him. Susanna does everything possible not to lay her hands among the snug fitting black shirt Brantley is wearing. Susanna finally places her hands against his chest only to push away from him. She leaves that man standing there with hunger in his eyes and a proud, sinful grin.

"Still didn't answer me about dinner, darlin in all that fussing you did," Brantley taunts Susanna while sliding his hands into his jeans. She tries to find something to occupy herself behind the counter, but Brantley just strolls back into her personal space. I quietly step more into the corner nibbling on my breakfast. Meh, I had a few minutes to spare before I had to be at work. I usually try not to get involved in town gossip, but this morning has told me something has gone down in this town that I've missed. Susanna answers my inner curiosity when she slams her palms down on the counter. Brantley doesn't even flinch at her temper.

"For God's sake, Brantley! It's bad enough we are the reason for the church sermon yesterday! Can you just stop?!" Susanna exclaims. I almost choke on my breakfast whipping Susanna's head around Brantley. Her cheeks tint before giving a bashful smile. At that moment, Brantley tilts her chin to face him directly.

"Hmm, did we?" He lowly replies just enough for me to still overhear. That man's voice sends a whimper trembling out of Susanna's mouth that even from the angle I'm standing has Brantley's full attention. "I was too busy making sure I didn't get hit between a flying hymnal and Mama's hand." I lose it. My giggling has both Brantley and Susanna give their attention to me standing in the corner. I crumple up my trash wiping my hand on a napkin before I head for the door. He gives me a grin and then turns back towards Susanna. I can hear the fuming from her nostrils all the way across the shop. "So what will it be, Susanna? Take you to dinner when I come back to town? That bus out there waiting to take me to Nashville won't wait forever."

Brantley's POV

I flopped down onto the couch in the studio letting out a deep, tired sigh. Between still touring and working on this next album I was desperate for some downtime. My mind wandered to the auburn haired woman back home that was giving me a sweet tooth. I should have gotten her number before I left. I pulled my phone out of my pocket sending Ben a text to get that from Tiffany for me. Being glutton for punishment I guess after how my year had been going, I flipped through finding the picture Kolby had sent teasing me that he was getting his cupcake order while I was out of town.

Even in jeans, a Jefferson Dragons t-shirt covered by an apron, Susanna was just so damn effortlessly beautiful it took my breath away. But the way my luck with women ran I was better off being a bachelor. Something about her just tugged at me once I laid eyes on her again. More I thought back through the haze of my partying years, I had seen her around just hadn't paid close attention. But at the time even if I had made a play for her, she didn't need to be tangled up with the likes of me.

The fire in her amber eyes glaring at me in church this past Sunday with that hymn book slightly raised. She was for sure going to nail me in the head with it if Mrs. Connie hadn't stopped her. Coach Hale had smothered a laugh behind his hand seeing the interaction between me and his baby girl. When she had started high school the entire baseball team and half the football team had been threatened to leave her alone. Wonder what his thoughts of me trying to date his darlin daughter now would be. Do remember the man having an impressive gun collection.

I checked through my email as I waited for Dann to finish listening to this latest playback. There were still a few songs I had to finish tweaking before we recorded them. Scott had assured me we had plenty time since the tentative release date was during the second quarter of next year. One email caught my eye making me groan in frustration. I jerked my head up glaring at my manager idly sitting on the other end of the couch typing on his laptop. I growled making Rich turn his head.

"Dammit Rich," I grumbled seeing a smile twitch at his lips. "I told you I needed some down time and now you schedule something on my break. I know I will be back and forth to Nashville working on the album. I'm tired man."

"Hmmm..." Rich said with a chuckle never looking up still pecking away. "I think if you look a little closer BG, something tells me you won't be bitching. Not after what Ben told me when I mentioned it earlier. And nope, no backing out for either you or Luke. I am not going against Kerri. Woman will have all three of our balls on a platter."

I sighed rubbing my hand along my chin reading the email. The further along I got the broader my grin spread. Oh, well now. This explained why Susanna was so damn aggravated the day I left. This little raffle just added

to it after what had happened at church the day before. I suddenly couldn't
wait to get home now. I got to help out a great charity, chance to more
than likely hang with Luke some since he would be in town and maybe,
just maybe get Susanna to say yes to a date.

Little over a week later, I stepped out under the awning covering the door
leading into Susanna's bakery with a grin on my face. The rain that had
obviously soaked the brunette who had hurried in, was starting to slack off.
I knew Susanna had wanted to get Luke to meet the mother of the little girl
who had been drawn for the hunt with him. A grin spread across my lips
as I pulled my keys out of my pocket heading to my truck to wait on Luke.
Couldn't help but whistle as I walked while I schemed in my mind trying
to figure out a date that with the possibility to sweep little Miss Susanna
Hale off her feet.

Giving The Preacher New Material

I nervously adjusted the bronze lace dress that had rushed out to buy earlier today mid freak out. I had a black jacket and heels that would go with it. Honestly, I had been a little shocked to receive a text from Brantley earlier today asking me to be ready at seven and to dress up. I bit my lip fluffing the soft curls Tiffany had insisted on doing my hair in before she had darted out of my house. She acted like I hadn't been on a date in forever. Okay, maybe she was right. Just hadn't been interested. I was honestly scared to get interested now. Little intimidating to get a date with your high school crush. Even if I had steadily refused at first. I slipped my jacket on about the time headlights swept through my front windows. I puffed out a breath reaching for my purse making sure I had cash and my cellphone.

A knock on my door sounded a second later. I pulled it open trying to keep my gasp in. While the man did look hot as hell was not expecting to see the outlaw of Jefferson High standing there in a black dinner jacket, black button up shirt underneath, dark blue jeans without holes and a big grin.

Of course that ever present hat was there. Just what was he up to. He held out a red rose that I knew by sight to be from the bushes outside the library. Guess it was the thought that counted right?

"Damn darlin," Brantley murmured as I turned to lay the rose on the table near the door grabbing my keys giving him a nervous smile. Eyes trailed from the top of my curled hair to the tips of my heels making me a little taller. "You look beautiful."

"Thank you," I said with a shy smile shutting the door slipping my keys into my purse. "Clean up pretty well yourself. Totally not a look I was expecting."

"It happens from time to time," he chuckled opening the passenger door of his truck holding out his hand to help me climb in. His mama did raise a gentleman for sure hellraiser or not. "Careful climbing in darlin. Don't slip on the running bar with your heels. Which make your legs look amazing by the way."

"My eyes are up here Gilbert," I said with a laugh making him grin as he shut the door. He climbed in the driver's seat shaking his head rolling his eyes.

"Starting to sound like your damn daddy," he laughed as I threw my head back laughing. "Busting my balls already."

We headed out of my street easing through town music playing as we drove. I was about to say something when Brantley stopped at the last red light on the road headed to Athens and I almost swallowed my tongue as I glanced out the window.

"Shit!" I yelped ducking my head.

"Susie Q, you okay?" Brantley asked as I dared a glance at him. God, this light needed to change to green. I pointed to the pickup next to us seeing his head turn then he burst out laughing. Of course the preacher and his wife would be in the vehicle beside us. Sweet baby Jesus he would be changing his sermon again this week. Kill me now. A warm hand settled on my arm. "Want me to roll the window down so you can wave?" I hissed at him baring my teeth as his hand slid down to squeeze mine. "My windows are tinted sweetheart. Think you are safe. Hate to have to dodge flying hymns or heaven help me the Bible too tomorrow morning."

"Ass," I grumbled smacking his arm as the light turned green. "It's not that I am ashamed to be on a date with you."

"I get it," he grinned. "Being the topic of the town gossip mill once in the last couple of weeks is enough. I understand."

We made idle talk the drive into Athens. I was surprised when Brantley pulled into the parking lot of Porterhouse Grill. Well that explained the need to dress up. I would have been happy with Waffle House but I had heard this place's desserts were beyond amazing. Their pastry chef had studied in France. A dream of mine that I hadn't been able to do. The hostess led us to a table making eyes at Brantley the whole time making me struggle to keep from rolling my. Swear it was like high school all over again. But his eyes never wavered from me, even pulling my chair out. After that is when it seemed to go downhill a little. While the dinner was delicious, the random small talk okay, I noticed Brantley tugging at the collar of his shirt a little more as time went on. Then nervous tapping of his fingers on the table. Poor man was miserable.

"You okay over there?" I asked taking another bite of my chocolate mousse cake trying not to moan at the fluffy taste. Piercing green eyes narrowed at me after he swallowed the bite he had just taken.

"I'm fine," Brantley said raising an eyebrow at me. I glanced around the low-lit restaurant with the white table clothes and shrugged. I winced praying I didn't look ungrateful. It wasn't that at all. This was just the place you came to celebrate a milestone anniversary or something. Not a first date. At least for me. "What Susanna, I can't treat a beautiful woman to a nice dinner?"

"Even if you are miserable doing it?" I countered back seeing his lips flatten. Ah ha, caught him. "It's a very sweet gesture BG. Really, thank you. Dinner was delicious. But a nice dinner doesn't always have to be somewhere like this. A place with a reservation. Overpriced food even if it is good. It could be a picnic or a steakhouse where you aren't expected to wear a jacket and I don't have to wear a dress and heels.

"But what if you look beautiful in the dress," he murmured reaching over to lay his hand on top of mine making me blush. Then a panty dropping smirk spread across his lips making me feel a cross between wanting to kiss him and smack him.

"Still the cocky bad boy," I grumbled seeing him frown at me but I didn't move my hand from under his. "I said yes didn't I?"

"Only to get me to leave," Brantley said with a chuckle squeezing my hand then moving it to take care of the check the waiter had just brought. He rolled his eyes. "That was after you tried to shove a cookie down my throat. Don't tell Mama, but yours are even better than hers."

"Well you were causing a scheme," I snapped back shaking a finger at him as he stood up pulling my chair out. Hands brushed my shoulders as he helped me into my jacket moving my hair out of the way causing me to shiver. "In my place of business no less." Brantley settled a hand along the small of my back guiding me to the door both of us stepping out into the cool night. "Besides, if you had asked anyone they could have told you I prefer to be in jeans and a hoodie."

"Ok darlin, okay," he laughed tossing an arm around my shoulders guiding me to the truck. Lips brushed against my ear as he leaned down the chuckle sending tingles down my spine. His cologne teasing my nose making my mouth water. "Swear there is a firecracker under that quiet demeanor. I don't remember you being like this in high school."

"Maybe I was," I sassed back looking up at him. "But then again you would have never known. Always chasing some cheerleader from another school."

Brantley stopped walking look down at me thoughtfully for a second. He pulled his keys out dropping his arm and opened my door for me then helped me climb in. A half smile on his full lips as he paused in shutting the door leaning closer to me.

"Maybe I did," he said quietly. "But darlin, you were too young for me back then and yea I noticed."

I gasped as he shut the door then rounded the front of the truck. My question flew from my lips as soon as he climbed in. "What do you mean I was too young?" I asked him as he started the engine giving me a quick smile. I always assumed he never noticed me at all. Tiffany had been the outgoing one of the two of us.

"When we were in high school darlin," Brantley said shaking his head. "The crowd I was starting to run with, probably a good thing I kept my distance. That and your dad threatened the hell out of all of us." My mouth dropped open as he raised an eyebrow at me. I remember being sooooo embarrassed and so pissed off at Daddy for doing that. I was lucky to even get my first date that year. And it sure as hell hadn't been from any of the football or baseball players either. He grinned at me. "I was somewhat of a punk back then and no good for you Suzie Q. Besides you were fifteen and that would have gotten me into allll kinds of trouble."

"You know," I snickered poking his shoulder. "Was funny as hell that after-noon watching Darren load you into the back of the car because you had given the damn deputy a run for his money. Daddy had laughed when he told him you'd had Ken on the run across the county line."

"Shit," Brantley groaned shaking his head looking over at me with a wince. "You saw that? See, see what I was telling you."

"Welllll yea," I drawled with a giggle. Swore I saw his cheeks blush in the glow of the dashboard light. "Errrrryyyyyyybody saw that." I rolled my eyes. "You expect me to believe that you even knew who I was back then."

"I did," Brantley argued back with a laugh. I felt some of the tension from earlier seeping away. "Always so cute and quiet. Loved to bake even back then. I swear over half of the football team followed their nose to your dad's office on game day. You and Tiff were always inseparable."

"Just what every woman wants to hear," I groaned leaning my head back on the seat and groaning. "That they are cute. Yep she and I haven't changed in that aspect."

"Susanna," Brantley murmured quietly laying a hand on mine lacing our fingers together. The cool metal of his rings feeling odd along my warm skin. Made me wonder what they would feel like trailing elsewhere on my body. I crossed my legs clenching my thighs at the thought. "I knocked my own brother out of the way to hurry over to talk to you a couple of weekends ago. Made my eyes bug out of my head with the woman you grew up to be. Yes, I thought you were cute back then, but you take my breath away now."

I gasped looking out the windshield as we approached the city limits of Jefferson. I felt my cheeks burning with a blush as he squeezed my hand. I couldn't help but giggle.

"Well now," I said turning my head to give him a grin. "Don't you know how to turn a date around with an actual honest compliment."

"Darlin," he laughed shaking his head. "If you haven't figured it out before now let me fill you in baby girl. I am always honest. Very real and don't know how to be any other way."

"Really," I teased raising an eyebrow at him. "Yea, a fancy dinner is the real you? While I am grateful for the thought, we both know you weren't exactly relaxed tonight either."

"Well then," Brantley said huskily as he eased down Main street giving me a smirk. "Want to help me relax."

"Oh come on," I scoffed playfully. "I know you can do better than that."

"Hmmm,' he teased squeezing my hand lifting it to his lips brushing a soft kiss along my knuckles making my heart race. "Someone is gonna make me work for it."

"Did you think I was still a star struck fifteen-year-old girl?" I asked with a wink as he pulled in my driveway. "I'm not. I've grown up."

"Why darlin," he drawled putting the truck in park and letting his eyes trail over me. "Yes you most certainly have." I bit my lip looking at my front door then back at him. "Guess I should walk you to the door huh."

"Or..." I murmured making his eyes widen. "I do happen to have some of those chocolate chip cookies made. Maybe a few of those and a movie? What do you think?"

"And what about the preacher's wife walking her dog down the street?" Brantley teased making me laugh as he leaned an arm on the console looking at me. "I mean, she is definitely going to see us."

"Well you know," I whispered leaning a little closer to him seeing his eyes flare with arousal. God the things just him looking at me did to me. "Small town life and all. Already the talk of the town if you can't live it down might as well live it up."

"Hmm..." Brantley laughed shaking his head and letting go of my hand to open the door and climb out. "That is such an accurate description. Maybe why I used it as a song lyric. Movie and cookies sound like a plan."

Soooo he finally got his date. Thank you to both and for being evil on me with this one. She may or may not have a POV from one and only Mama Becky in her latest update of Crash My Party

Sin In Plain View

Susanna's POV

Taking one last look into the visor mirror of my Jeep, I made sure my hair was arranged around the edges of my neck. I blushed thinking about the patch of beard burn I had discovered there this morning. Last night, well last night had been interesting. I had laughed until my sides hurt at least until a pair of lips that tasted like chocolate captured mine. Shaking my head to clear my thoughts, I slid out heading across the church parking lot listening to my heeled brown leather boots click.

I wisely sidestepped the preacher's wife who was talking to my former first grade teacher. I held my head high, but my ears perked up at the mention of that Collins girl seen picking up her car this morning. My lips twisted in a smile wondering just what Sadie had been up to last night. I was gonna have to find out since Brantley had admitted he ditched on hanging out with Luke to go out with me. Spotting my parents sitting behind Tiffany, my steps faltered just a little seeing Ms. Becky sitting beside my mama. Crap! I should have just been late for church again. Mustering up some courage, I stepped into the empty pew behind them leaning down to kiss Daddy on the cheek trying to hear Mama's hushed conversation.

"Morning pumpkin," Daddy said looking back at me with a smile. "How was your date last night?"

"Daddddyyyy," I whined making him chuckle. Two pair of eyes with wide smiles met me as I stood up straight. "Morning Mama. Morning Ms. Becky."

"Good morning," Ms. Becky said with a grin giving me a wink that made me blush. "Hope your date went well."

"Have to fill me in later," Mama giggled as I sighed walking to the pew in front of them sitting down in the middle by Tiffany. She grinned at me as I rolled my eyes hearing the hushed giggles behind us. I swear those two were planning a wedding already. It had been one date. I pressed my fingers to my lips thinking about that last long kiss goodnight. Tiffany batted her blue eyes at me making me growl as she leaned closer to me.

"I want details on said date as well. Specifically of what BG thought of that dress," she murmured poking my arm. I couldn't help but blush remembering the look in his eyes when I opened the door. No doubt the damn man had been wondering what it would like rumpled on the floor instead of on me. "Honestly surprised you are here this morning. Figured you would still be tangled up in some sheets."

"Hush Tiff," I hissed rolling my eyes. "It went okay. Was an interesting night."

"Just bet it was," she snickered then elbowed me as a figure moved out of the corner of my eye. Sadie slid into the pew beside me in a cute pair of leggings with a top. Looking dressy and comfortable but no doubt catching a few eyes for wearing pants. The dark sunglasses still on her eyes made my lips twitch.

"Rough night Sadie dear," I whispered leaning closer to her getting a growl in return. "How did the hunting trip go yesterday? Ryleigh have fun."

"She had a blast," Sadie sighed slipping off her glasses dropping them into the purse near her feet. Ohh bless her the slight hangover was apparent. Tiffany sat her chin on my shoulder listening intently. Sadie gave us both an unsure look before continuing. "Luke was great with her. It's umm...."

"What can we say," Tiffany said with a wink. "Those Georgia country boys have a way of getting under your skin." She elbowed my side making a grin twist at Sadie's lips. "And out of your clothes."

Sadie broke out in a fit of coughing prompting Mama to reach up patting her back. Three purses opened in the pew in front of us as some of the ladies from the Red Hat Society passed pieces of peppermint back. Sadie blushed then accepted them. I was about to ask her to elaborate when a squeal came from the back where the teenage girls were known to congregate. Turning my head, I saw what the ruckus was all about. Now there was a fan girl's dream strolling into church side by side. No signature hat on for either of them this morning knowing that Mama Becky would tan their hides.

But Luke's blue and red plaid shirt fit just right as his eyes combed the congregation no doubt for the woman sitting beside me. Brantley may have his leather jacket on but the button up shirt on underneath would keep him out of trouble with his mama. Like a man on a mission, Brantley made a beeline for the pew we were sitting on with Luke in tow. He stopped at the end with a grin making half the heads in the front half of the sanctuary whip around. Shit. I narrowed my eyes at him only making that grin widen.

"Morning Mama, Mrs. Connie, Coach," he said. "It's a lovely day today isn't it." Sadie covered a laugh with her hand as Tiffany shook her head at him laying it on thick. Luke's lips twisted up in a sultry smile as Sadie finally lifted her head meeting his. Brantley slid into the pew patting Sadie on the shoulder. "Excuse me Sadie darlin." Tiffany scooted down the other direction while Sadie moved closer to the aisle leaving him plenty of room to settle down beside me. A long arm stretched out to rest along my back on the pew.

Fingers brushing along my shoulder making my skin feel like it was on fire thinking about them tangled in my hair last night. Like he was remembering, Brantley twirled the ends of my straightened hair absently as Luke settled down beside Sadie like there wasn't a ton of room left on the pew. Her mama was turned around with a grin and oh so blatantly getting a look at Luke from three rows ahead of us. A throat clearing behind us had Brantley's fingers stilling. He turned his head looking back with a sheepish grin before lifting his arm from around me. "Sorry Coach."

Luke leaned in to whisper something in Sadie's ear making her blush as a warm hand settled on my knee resting above the top of my boot. God help me this man was trying to kill me. Nothing more than some good old fashion, okay very intense kissing had happened last night, but didn't stop Brantley's lips or fingers from finding every patch of skin not concealed by my dress. The smell of his cologne teasing my nose making my mouth water as he leaned in near my ear.

"This dress looks almost as amazing as the one you were wearing last night," he murmured making sure his lips brushed my ear. I involuntarily shivered feeling goose bumps breaking out along my skin. "Would love to see you in nothing but those boots."

"Son," Mama Becky said from behind us making me jump trying to steer my thoughts away from telling him let's just skip church and make that happen. She leaned forward resting a hand on my shoulder. "Get that jacket off right now and give it to this sweet girl. Seems she has gotten a chill. Why they have the air conditioner on I don't know." A yelp from Luke made me smother a laugh as she thumped him in the back of the head. "Get that smirk off your face Thomas. I know you know how to behave in church. About time you made your presence known baby boy."

I turned my head to the right seeing Kolby slip into the pew on the other side of Tiffany. He winked at his mama before looking down the pew at the rest of us with a smirk. Brantley rolled his eyes as he shrugged out of his leather jacket draping it over me. My eyes widened as his hand slipped under the jacket still resting on my knee. Just a tad higher this time.

"Well look what we have here," he chuckled. "What exactly did I miss by going to Atlanta last night?"

"Let me fill you in Kolby," Tiffany giggled as the opening music started. She leaned over murmuring in his ear. I felt a calloused thumb swirl patterns on the bare skin of my thigh getting higher with each stroke. I cut my eyes at Brantley only to see him staring straight ahead humming along to the hymn. Kolby let out a laugh looking down the pew at the four of us wiggling his eyebrows. Daddy reached up smacking him in the back of the head.

"Thank you Mark," Mama Becky chuckled behind us lowly. "I couldn't reach him."

As the hymns went on the warm hand on my thigh continued stroking a path down to my knee and back up to my thigh teasing under the hem of my dress. I couldn't help it I squirmed in my seat shifting my leg trying to get him to stop. What does Brantley do, lightly smacks my leg making me gasp. Tiffany cuts her eyes at me biting her lip. Was he seriously going to sit here and try to fool around in church? That's it, I was officially going to hell. Between last night and his teasing me now, I was on edge needing something.

The ass was doing this on purpose. Could my panties actually be set on fire during the middle of church? Why yes they could because said teasing hand slid higher to brush a knuckle over the damp lace of them making me hide a moan behind a cough. I swallowed a whimper of disappointment when he rested his hand back on my knee as the preacher started to preach. On gossip and judgment no less.

Later, I let out a frustrated scream throwing my spatula across the kitchen of the silent bakery. I wiped at my face knowing the tears brimming in my eyes wouldn't help anything. Halloween was Thursday. One of my big ovens going out on me Friday putting me so far behind on my orders for later this week I was barley catching up after it being fixed this morning. I had hardly slept all weekend trying to do what I could from home. The gray sundress I had put on at lunch time to go to the Rotary Club luncheon was at least cooler in this hot kitchen than my jeans would have been. It, my hair, and apron had specks of flour and orange icing all over it. My auburn hair was up in a messy haphazard bun.

Then top things off, after kissing me after church that day I hadn't seen nor heard from Brantley. I was too dang prideful to ask Kolby when he had come in the other day with their dad. If he wanted to be this way then okay then. A quiet knock on the back door made a yelp sound in my throat. Figuring it was Stephanie bringing me some dinner that Mama had left over, I called for her to come in as I resumed my task of transferring cookies to a cooling rack with a new spatula.

"Just sit it on the counter Steph," I murmured not looking back. "I'll eat when I get time."

"What do you mean you haven't eaten?" I heard growled in my ear as arms wrapped around my waist making me stiffen. "Darlin, you look dead on your feet." I threw my elbow back into the chest of the man holding me resisting the urge to stomp my bare foot. I was not going to feel like I was back in high school wondering why the boy didn't call. I didn't have time for this shit. Brantley let out a hiss spinning me around gripping my arms narrowing his eyes at me. "What the fuck was that for Suzie Q? Did I do something to piss you off?"'

"Nope," I said coolly before ducking out of his arms. I turned my back to him again. "I am just busy. I don't have time for your games tonight."

"Games?" Brantley asked leaning against the counter beside me crossing his arms over his chest. "How about you just say what you really mean darlin."

"Fine!" I snapped shaking my head putting a hand on my hip. "You just up and disappear with no call or anything. Well fool me once BG. You know what never mind. It's none of my business. It was just a date so who gives a fuck what you have or who you have been up to."

"Shit," he muttered closing his eyes then opening them giving me an apologetic look. It was then I noticed the backwards camouflage hat, camo pants and t-shirt. A faint trace of face paint on his cheeks. A big hand reached out cupping my cheek. "I am so sorry darlin. It was Brantley week as my buddy Michael Lee calls it. I've been hunting and the camp has shitty cell reception which is why I didn't call. It slipped my mind to even mention it before I left town. I told Kolby to tell you for me if he came in because I left headed to Michael's in such a hurry. I should have called you myself."

"No worries," I muttered rolling my eyes. "I don't need an explanation. You're a grown man. Do whatever you want."

"It's a courtesy sweetheart," he growled back leaning his head closer to mine. "Because I sure as fuck would want some answers if you up and disappeared on me after one date. I was headed straight to your house to see you before going home but I saw your Jeep still parked in the lot when I drove by. Not good for you to be here so late by yourself."

"I can take care of myself," I argued back tiredly. The concern I saw reflecting back at me in the narrowed green eyes staring me down unnerved me. Clearing my throat, I moved my head away from Brantley's. "Listen I've got to finish these orders before I can even stop for the night okay. I'm behind as it is. Just call me tomorrow or something okay."

"No," Brantley snapped grabbing the spatula out of my hands reaching around me for the ties of my apron. A surprised gasped bubbled out. "I'm taking you home Susanna you are dead on your feet. This can wait."

"No it can't!" I yelled shaking my heavy feeling head in frustration. "Dammit Brantley this is my business."

"Yea well you can't run it if you can't function from lack of sleep!" he yelled back getting in my face. The back door swung open revealing my cousin Stephanie strolling in with narrowed eyes. Her auburn hair identical to mine pulled back away from her face.

"He's right," she said slamming the door making my head drop in shame. "You have worked your ass off the last few days. I'll stay up tonight filling these orders. Josh is coming in to open in the morning letting me catch a nap. Between him and Cheyenne they can handle the morning rush. BG, take her home. Make sure she doesn't step foot in town until lunchtime or even at all tomorrow. Go rest Sus. I've got you covered. I'll call Aunt Connie if I need help."

"But..." I started to argue as Stephanie shoved purse at me pointing at the door. Brantley chuckled wrapping an arm around my waist. I stomped my foot glaring at him with a hiss making his lips flatten. I almost took a step back. "Fine! I'll go home. I'll be back at two Steph."

"No you won't," Brantley chuckled grabbing my waist and throwing me over his shoulder. "You are gonna relax."

"But my Jeep," I persisted as Stephanie waved goodbye. Her head tossed back with a cackle that rivaled the Wicked Witch. A rumbling laugh sounded into the quiet night as Brantley strode towards his truck.

"It will be fine here darlin," he assured me. "No one will question it being parked here and my house is well off the road so no one near to see you walk into my house. See, no sermon about you this week."

Well well....someone just got the foot put down on them. Wonder what can do to relax?? I know Sadie should be. That's coming isn't it ......

Takin A Break

Brantley's POV

I ran a tired hand over my face taking a left into my driveway hitting the button on my visor for the gates. Glancing over, I saw Susanna dozing with her cheek against the window. She was probably going to be pissed that I didn't take her home, but she would get over it. I wanted my bed after being gone and if she was out here I could make sure there was no trying to sneak back to the bakery. Climbing out of the truck, I walked around gently opening the door. Amber colored eyes flew open as I chuckled wrapping an arm around her lifting her out of the truck. Susanna swayed on her feet once they touched the concrete. Slim fingers twisted into my shirt trying to keep herself up right.

"Come on sweetheart," I told her gently banding my arm around her waist guiding her towards the house. Kolby came bounding out the front door whistling headed to his truck. See his crashed here while I was gone. He stopped seeing me then his lips twisted up in a smirk seeing Susanna. I growled at him making her jump. "I have a bone to pick with you later little brother. Forget to deliver a message?"

"Oops," Kolby said with a grin passing by us. "Slipped my mind. Look I gotta go take ol' girl out for a movie. Should have called big brother!"

"He's got a point," I swore I heard Susanna mutter but chose to ignore it. She was right but hell if I would tell her that. Honestly, was used to being on my own again so I hadn't thought about it. Guiding her into the house, I shut the front door locking it before lacing my fingers with hers tugging her towards the stairs. She leaned heavily into my side as we walked. Opening the door to my bedroom, I eased Susanna down to sit on the end of the big bed.

"Wait right here," I told her softly. "I'll go get the shower started for you. Then you are crashing."

"I'm not two Brantley," Susanna scoffed rolling her eyes before laying back on my bed closing her eyes. "I'm just tired not an invalid."

"I am well aware you aren't a child," I snarled clenching my fists in frustration. I stalked over leaning down to brace my hands on either side of her head making Susanna's eyes fly open. My boots bumped against her bare feet dangling off the bed. I lowered my head hovering over her lips. "How about you stop fighting me for five minutes and let someone take care of you for a change. You do for everyone else but yourself Susanna. Ask anyone in town and they will readily agree to that." Pressing my lips to hers, I heard a whimper bubble out of her throat. As I increased the pressure of my lips, arms reached up wrapping around my neck trying to pull me down on the bed with her. With a chuckle, I broke the kiss hearing her growl at me as I stood up taking my hat off tossing it on my dresser. "Not tonight sweetheart. You need some sleep."

"No what I need is some relief from your relentless teasing!" Susanna snapped sitting up to prop on her elbows glaring at me. She closed her amber eyes in mortification. "Shit, I said that out loud didn't I?"

"Yes you did," I snickered turning to head towards the bathroom. "I may be a lot of things baby girl, but a tease is not one of them." I walked over to the walk-in shower turning the water on both ends making sure it was on hot. Seeing the water start to steam, I stepped into my closest grabbing a t-shirt for Susanna and kicked my boots off. I walked back into my room seeing her glare at me. With a chuckle, I pulled her to her feet kissing her quickly. God, she always tasted and smelled like vanilla cupcakes. Like the smell was permanently etched into her skin. Breaking the kiss, I smacked her ass lightly pointing towards the door. "In you go. There is a t-shirt for you laying on the counter. I'll grab one when you get done."

"Or," Susanna walked forward swaying her hips reaching back for the zipper on the dress letting it fall to the floor. I bit my bottom lip as smooth tan skin encased in steel gray lace appeared. And God help me that thong showed off her toned ass perfectly. For someone so sleepy, the sexy smirk Susanna shot me over her shoulder as she paused in the doorway letting that lace bra drift to the floor. "I could use some help washing my back. That is unless you are too tired outlaw."

Where in hell had this come from? Dead on her feet one second now a flirty minx the next. I stood there in shock running a hand over my face as she disappeared. Even if she would be mad, the gentlemanly thing to do would be to leave her alone. Yea. That's what I would do I thought staring at my boots noting the zipper to my camo pants getting a little too tight. Then I heard a giggle as a tiny pair of lace thongs landed at my feet followed by humming in the shower. Fuck it! That's it! I had to get my hands on her. Tugging my t-shirt over my head I tossed it to the floor before unzipping my pants kicking them off as I walked. I almost tripped over my own two feet seeing Susanna's back to me bracing her hands on the tile wall letting the hot water cascade over her skin.

Opening the glass door, I stepped in shutting it softly. My eyes trailing over the woman in front of me making my mouth water. My fingers itch to trail over that smooth skin. Smart thing to have done would have been to run as far away from her as possible. Last thing a good girl like her needed was to get tangled up with a guy like me. That thought didn't stop my arms from wrapping around her waist pulling her back into my chest. A gasp bubbled out from her feeling how hard I was just from looking at her. Wet, auburn hair brushed along my shoulder. Gliding my hands up, I cupped her breasts coaxing a low moan to sound out. Susanna's small hands came up gripping my wrists as I rolled a nipple between my fingers.

"Shit," she hissed lolling her head to look up at me. The pure flaming desire in her amber eyes almost sending me to my knees. My hands following her curves like a roadmap learning her body. "God that feels good."

"Does it now?" I asked huskily leaning down grazing my teeth over her tanned shoulder feeling her shiver. Letting my thoughts get the better of me, I turned Susanna around in my arms raising my hands to cup her cheeks. The stress lines and dark circles under her beautiful eyes gave me pause. "This isn't why I brought you out here darlin. As much as..."

"Let me fill you in on something," Susanna murmured using my forearms as leverage to stand on her tip toes molding her chest to mine. Hard nipples pressed against me as she bit my bottom lip coaxing a growl from my throat. She was playing with fire. A smooth leg lifted hooking around my hip. I had no doubt if I looked down between us I'd find a warm, bare pussy just begging to be fucked. "I might look like the cute girl next door, but I've got a tad more of a naughty wild side than you think."

"Fuck me yes you do," I gasped feeling lips trail up my neck sinking into my ear tugging slightly. Digging my fingers into Susanna's hips I lifted her up capturing her lips as I slowly walked forward pressing her back against the cool tile. Grinding my hips into hers brushing my hard dick along her core feeling the heat making my heart pound. No doubt she was soaking wet and dripping that had nothing to do with the shower. Nails scored down my back as sucked on my tongue trying to get closer.

Kissing her the other the night and not bending her over that couch had taken all the self control I possessed. I wanted nothing more right now than to drive into her warm center taking her over the edge again and again. Had been thinking about spreading her out across my kitchen island in nothing but one of those aprons she wore at the bakery the whole time I had been gone hunting. Lowering my head, I tugged a dusky pink nipple between my teeth clamping them down gently making Susanna mewl so damn prettily my cock ached at the sound.

"Now," she murmured hoarsely blinking warm water out of her eyes as I raised my head looking down at her. "I need you now. No more teasing. No more playing. I need you to fuck me til I scream."

"Well then," I chuckled darkly sliding my hand palm down between us pressing my thumb to her aching clit. Her head slumped to my shoulder her chest heaving as I rubbed vigorously making her gasp clawing at my shoulder. My hips pinning her in place as I reached down lifting her then guiding my hard dick into her aching center kissing her deeply. I stopped just as the head passed her entrance breaking the kiss. "Wait...need.."

"Pill!" Susanna whimpered flinging her head back with a gasp. "On the pill we are good. Jesus Brantley now!"

Shifting my hips, I drove up into her wet core groaning at the snug fit feeling her tighten around me. I stilled letting Susanna adjust opening my opens to stare into hers. The pure ecstasy in her amber orbs turned me on even more. Something else I felt staring into them gave me pause. The vulnerability of falling for her. I couldn't do it. Have mutual fun for both of us yes. Because I enjoyed being around her but guard my heart against anything else. Nails tracing down my spine sinking into my ass urged me on as I started a punishing rhythm bucking my hips up with the intent of doing what she asked. That was to scream my name.

Bracing one hand on the shower wall, I took my other burying my fingers into wet, silky auburn hair tugging it back baring Susanna's throat to me leaning down to suck hard against the curve feeling her grow wetter. Hard nipples brushed my chest with each stroke. God, what was this woman doing to me. It was the fact of going bareback. That was it. That was all it was. Toes dug into my thighs finding purchase to raise her hips along with mine chasing the same precipice of pleasure we were both heading towards.

I swirled my hips driving up hard feeling wet molten heat clamp around me feeling the shudders and quakes of her orgasm. Made me harder hearing Susanna scream my name. That desperate keening wail sending a trigger through my system pulling my orgasm from me flooding her pussy with hot ropes of cum. Couldn't help it. My knees buckled sending us both to the tile floor with water cascading over us.

"Holy fuck," Susanna whimpered against my heaving chest. A chuckle slipped past my lips a second later as her eyes lifted to meet mine. Leaning down to kiss me she wound her arms around my neck. "Ask and you shall receive I guess."

"Well had to show you I was up to the task," I chuckled smoothing her hair away from her face blinking water from my eyes. "How about we get cleaned up and you get some of that rest you promised Stephanie you would get."

"Only," she purred biting my lip with a quiet laugh. "If I get a repeat of that after I get some sleep."

"Hmm..." I said pretending to think about it climbing to my wobbly feet reaching down for her. A light smack across her ass had her jumping. "I might could be convinced."

Next morning a quiet sigh pulled me from my sleep. I opened my eyes to see auburn hair draped across my shoulder onto my chest and a pair of amber colored eyes glaring at me slightly. Surely after last night and waking her up at dawn this morning there was no way this woman was mad at me. Smoothing my hand from her hip to Susanna's thigh under the sheets earned me a smack to my chest.

"Stop," she murmured poking her kiss swollen lips out at me. "I need to go check on things Brantley. I know what Stephanie said but...."

"No," I said shrugging my shoulders letting out a yawn.

"What do you mean no?" Susanna sassed back trying to wiggle out of my arms. "My phone is dead by now I'm sure. My keys, Jeep, and hell even my shoes are at work. I need you to take me please."

"Nope," I chuckled darkly rolling over to pin her beneath me kissing her slowly. Felt her body melt against mine. Lifting my head, I looked down at her with a soft smile. "Not going to work today. I will take you to get your Jeep later I do promise that. I understand you have to work tomorrow because it's a busy day. But today, no. We are gonna get up. Looks like a pretty fall day outside. I'll run you by your house to change clothes and get some shoes. You need jeans and a long sleeve shirt. Then we are coming back by here to leave the truck and taking the bike out. I might even let you pick which one. Won't hurt you to have a day of fun will it?"

"Finnnneeee," Susanna grumbled trying to keep the smile from teasing along her lips. "That's something I've never done before."

"Well then baby," I told her sitting up giving her a wink. "You are in for a treat. Let's go."

Hmmmmm....guess she is relaxed now.   but isn't there a question Miss Sadie is going to have to answer soon. Be interesting to see how that Sunday dinner turned out. Turn on over to Crash My Party to find out.

Highlight of Small Town Life

M rs. Ruby Johnson's POV (thank you)

I took a deep breath loving the smell of the fall air. The lovely golden leaves falling to the ground. Just enough chill in the air to keep away the mugginess of the South. Taking a sip of the coffee I had grabbed from One Hale of a Bakery, I looked down at my sweet little poodle Mitizi prancing along as we walked turning onto our street. Why I loved living close to Main Street. Close to everything and as Elmer would remind me, close to the gossip.

I had the signature pink bag of the bakery looped over my wrist with the Halloween cookies I had picked up for the trick or treaters tomorrow night. I had asked Stephanie where Susanna was. Not like her to not be there when I went into get my coffee while I was walking Mitizi. Hope the poor child wasn't sick. All Stephanie had done was bite her bottom lip and say that Susanna was getting some much deserved rest. That poor girl did work way too hard.

I guess I could give Connie a call when I got home to check on her. We'd been visiting the grandkids in Florida the last few weeks, so I was a little out of sorts on the news of the prayer chain. Elmer would snort, shake his paper, and tell me to admit I had missed out on the latest town gossip. I proceeded down our street with a pep in my step and a yip from Mitzi when a loud roar made me jump. My poor little angel darted back to hide around my legs shaking.

A black motorcycle zoomed by making me gasp. Why I never! Looking closer I recognized the rider with no problem. If that don't beat all I ever seen in this world. No good, no account for nothing, hoodlum oldest Gilbert boy. Bless his mama. I needed to say an extra prayer for her. Becky is a saint and no matter what she did he was a rotten apple at times. A hell raiser through and through. What had me spinning around almost tripping over Mitzi's leash was the woman on the back. A shock of auburn hair blowing in the wind. I could hear a booming laugh from Brantley as he stopped at the stop sign making my jaw almost hit the pavement.

Is that? Oh, I know I was not seeing Coach Hale's sweet little girl on that monstrosity of a death machine! I watched as he leaned back catching Susanna's lips in a slow kiss making even me blush for it being in broad daylight. Heavens to Betsy! They needed to be on the prayer list. Ughhh someone needs to talk to her. Just can't believe she is taking up with the likes of him.

Susanna's POV

I rubbed my hands along the sleeves of my navy blue sweater wishing I had grabbed my jacket out of my Jeep when Tiffany and I parked at the football field earlier. It was Friday night in the fall of course under these bright lights is where I would be. Highlight of small town life and a lot of times like a religion of its own. Mama had warned me it would get cooler as the sun went down. She was settled back in her chair rest with a red blanket over her knees. Decked out in Jefferson High regalia from head to toe looking every inch of a coach's wife.

When I was younger I had wanted to be just like her. Guess I was in some ways. Did have a crush on the starting quarterback back in the day. Was tied to this small town for sure with my business now. That faint dream of studying baking in France teased at the edge of my mind from time to time. But that is all it was, a dream. Tiffany reached over tugging on the bright red scarf I was wearing with a smirk leaning closer to me. Her long blonde hair pulled up in a high ponytail complete with bow from our cheerleading days. I had always been a little too shy to tryout until our senior year.

"Why the scarf Suz?" she whispered with a snicker. I felt my entire face turn red as I glared at her. "Got something to hide?"

"Don't know what you are talking about," I grumbled through clenched teeth forcing a smile on my face as Mrs. Ruby walked by holding onto the arm of her husband Elmer shaking her head at me. Well that was strange she always stopped and spoke normally. I elbowed Tiffany as she giggled. "Stop Tiff. I..."

"You are full of crap if you think I am gonna believe that," Tiffany laughed grabbing the ends of my hair lifting then looking closely letting out a whistle. "Well, I wasn't expecting teeth marks. Look at BG go."

"Girls," Mama said with a laugh shaking her head. She narrowed her eyes at the field not agreeing with a call Daddy had made. "He should have run the ball!" I saw her debate calling his phone before turning her attention back to us. Wouldn't be the first time. I swear she knew the playbook better than the quarterback. A slim hand reached over patting my jean clad leg. "I was actually surprised to see you alone tonight honey. Figured you would have a date or something."

"Mama," I sighed rolling my eyes. "We aren't dating or anything. It's not..."

"Guess it could be termed as hooking up," Tiffany chuckled making me whirl around and smack her arm. Mama sighed as we battled back and forth before Tiffany shrugged her shoulders. "Sorry Mrs. H."

"It's something,' Mama laughed poking my arm putting her two cents in. "That boy made a beeline for you in church. And someone's Jeep stayed parked in their own parking lot for not one, but two nights in a row. Your own daddy almost ran his truck off the street yesterday morning seeing you hop off the back of a motorcycle to run into work late. So Susanna darlin, however you want to term it, there is something going on between you and Brantley."

"Well when I know," I said with a laugh leaning over to kiss her cheek. "You will be the first to know."

"Oh sweetie," Mama chuckled turning her attention back to the game. "Becky and I will know before you two. Haven't you figured out how the small-town gossip works yet."

I settled back against the bleacher getting absorbed in the game. Had been part of my life for years. A pair of jean clad legs settled on either side of me before a black leather jacket slipped around my shoulders making me turn my head and look up. Felt my heart skip a beat seeing that backwards black hat and a wide smile as Brantley leaned down brushing a quick kiss across my lips.

"Sorry," he said with a sheepish shrug confusing me on why he was sorry. He hadn't mentioned anything about seeing me tonight when he'd come into the bakery after the lunch rush trying to sweet talk a dozen chocolate chip cookies out of me. "I had planned on being here sooner, but I got held up on a conference call with my manager and my label president. Working out studio dates." He leaned over wrapping a long arm around Mama's shoulders hugging her. "Evening Mrs. H. looking lovely as always."

"Brantley, son," Mama snickered rolling her eyes. "When did you become such a kiss ass? Afraid I'll still get Mark to make you run laps?"

"More like wondering if he has been cleaning his guns," Tiffany snickered shoving Brantley's arm making him wink at her. "I mean you are chasing after his baby girl."

"That I am," he laughed slumping down on the bleachers stretching out his legs. Arms wrapped around my shoulders pulling me back into his chest. I tamped down a content sigh feeling warmer than I had been earlier. I knew without a doubt Mama snuck at least one picture when we weren't looking that I am sure hit Ms. Becky's phone in a heartbeat. At least three girls from the class above me in school strolled by giving me dirty looks over who was sitting with their arms around me. Won't lie made me feel a little smug. Sorry ladies, your potential husband number two was busy with me tonight.

I bit my lip listening to the conversation flowing around me wondering in some ways how I got lucky for something I had wanted as a teenager to happen finally did. Mama would tell me that there is a time for everything in life. I guess she was right. A soft kiss brushing along my cheek made me blush as the preacher and his wife walked by. Mrs. Shelia didn't even try to hide her raised eyebrows. I wanted to snap at her to take a picture it would last longer but the couple following behind them had Tiffany's jaw dropping and the chest I was leaned against rumbling with a laugh.

"Well I guess that was ol' girl he was talking about the other night," Brantley chuckled as Kolby walked by with his arm resting around Kaylee Bryson making me roll my eyes. Tiffany visibly shuddered as Mama winced trying to keep a polite smile on her face.

"You need to have a talk with your little brother BG," Tiffany murmured rolling her eyes. "Kaylee is so not what he needs."

"What?" Brantley laughed looking at her as he idly played with my fingers. "It's Kolby and she is hot. He will be fine."

"Oh really now," I teased back at him for his comment turning my head meeting his eyes. "She's hot huh?"

"Gonna get something he can't get rid of more likely," Mama grumbled rolling her eyes. "Lord wait until your mama meets her."

"She won't," Brantley said with a snicker. "He ain't bringing anyone home for her scrutiny trust me." Mama cracked up laughing at that. Guess it was a good thing I already knew his mama even though I wasn't sure what was going on between us. Brantley leaned down nosing my hair away from my ear brushing his lips against it making me shiver. Suddenly I could care less about the football game and was more intent on getting out of here. The low timber to his voice sending dampness straight to between my thighs. "Trust me darlin. She has nothing on you and these tight jeans you are wearing. I'm trying to be good and not imagine what is on underneath them. But not doing any good. I have plans on getting you out of them later." I swallowed a moan and jerked when I heard a low growl slip past his lips.

I turned following his gaze down the bleachers to where Kenny Macon was sitting with a couple of his buddies from the soccer team in high school. Kenny had moved back earlier this year frequently dropping into my bakery asking for a date to make up for being an ass in high school. He had taken an interest in me our junior year. A date or two he had swept me off my sixteen-year-old feet. Tiffany had hated him and still did. But after getting all dressed up for the Homecoming dance that year, I had been stood up with my only choice for Mama and Daddy to drop me off at the school. Rumors were flying by the time I got there that Kenny was out with some other girl. Daddy had been none to pleased.

The asshat had surfaced at school on Monday though looking like hell with a busted lip, two black eyes, and a broken nose. Refused to tell anyone who had beaten his ass. We all were sure it was the girl's boyfriend. "I will tell you this much darlin. If he don't stop staring, he is about to get a refresher in why Eli and I spent used to shove him in a locker for fun our senior year. I never liked that little prick."

"Speaking of pricks," Tiffany said with a snort pointing towards the top above us at a group of guys passing a flask back and forth laughing obnoxiously. I shook my head and winced when I felt the grip Brantley had on my hands tighten. "That is asking for a drunk and disorderly in a heartbeat. God, what did I ever see in Jake Myers back in the day?"

"I told you he was a dick," I reminded her making Mama chuckle. I gasped recognizing Ryan Fitzmorris as the ringleader. His features stood out to me more than ever as I connected the dots of the rumors I had heard when Sadie moved to town. I had never asked but I had heard he was Ryleigh's father. "You see Ryan is right in the middle of it."

"I never liked that cocksucker," Brantley growled shooting a glare their way. Mama reached over smacking his arm. "Sorry Mrs. H, but he always rubbed me the wrong way. He gave the Chief more hell than I did."

"Hopefully he is just here for the game," Mama sighed shaking her head. "His little cousin in the starting tight end this year."

Later on after the game, Tiffany and I laughed standing on the sidelines watching the boys celebrate. That had included dumping the cooler on Daddy making him receive a smack from Mama for yelling "shit that's cold!". Standing near the fifty-yard line as the crowd started filtering away I was hit with a touch of nostalgia missing my high school days a little. Tiff threw her arm around my leather covered shoulders with a grin pointing over at Daddy. He spun a football around on his hand giving Brantley a wink laughing at something they were talking about with a couple seniors.

"I dunno son," Daddy boomed rolling his eyes playfully. "I don't think you still have it in you."

"Ohh that is a challenge," Brantley laughed taking the ball away from him and pointing at Benjamin, one of the wide receivers. Benjamin took off with a laugh as B jogged out on the field pulling back and launching it downfield straight into his waiting hands. I smiled watching him laughing throwing the ball around with some of the other boys. Daddy walked over leaning down to kiss my cheek with a smile.

"Yep that boy still has it Suzie Q," he chuckled crossing his arms over his chest. "You've got you a good one there even when he doesn't want to admit it."

"Not like that Daddy," I sighed making him laugh harder walking away to swing Mama up in his arms making her shriek.

"Keep tellin yourself that sweetie!" Daddy said shifting her over his shoulders making the team starting cheering. "Keep tellin yourself that!"

I let out a yelp being distracted by my parents when a pair of hands gripped my waist lifting me up to wrap my legs around them. Brantley gave me a big grin as I wrapped my arms around his neck.

"What do you say to getting out of here hmmm..." he murmured kissing me slowly.

"Thought you would never ask," I whispered back giving him a wink. "Let's go."

Little Friday night lights and hmmm wonder if that is all that Sadie's ex is in town for ?

Icing and Yelling

S usanna's POV

Late January 2014

I tapped my foot along with the song on the radio focusing on icing a cake to be stored in the freezer for next weekend. I had come in today to help Stephanie knowing it would be busy with the baseball tournament at Jefferson this weekend. Mama was of course front and center keeping the book for Daddy and ear tugging a freshman or two. Steph was manning the front while I got some work done back here. Brantley had been at the field watching the games with Kolby and was supposed to pick me up when we closed.

Things had been going good between us the last few months. Him surprising me with a trip out of town around New Year's had shocked me honestly. Then once realizing it was to New Orleans, the party capital of the south, well I had frowned. Not that I wasn't grateful for the gesture, just had seemed like a lot of thought not considered. But Brantley had steadily proved me wrong because I fell in love with the food in general. It may not be Paris but the thought that I would enjoy a place like that considering my profession and love of cooking made my heart melt. Like he had told me walking through the French Quarter, it may not be France because he knew how much I wanted to go, it was the best he could do on the spur of the moment.

Arms slid around my waist as lips trailed along the side of my neck making me shiver. My hand holding the icing bag shook when teeth grazed my ear. I closed my eyes feeling my breathing pick up.

"Think you can focus under pressure baby?" Brantley teased in my ear making me groan. He slid his hands under my apron toying with the waist of my jeans making me growl at him. He laughed backing away holding his hands up. "Yes mam. I will stop. Know I will be banned from cookies if I don't."

"Damn right mister," I grinned standing on my tip toes to kiss him. He turned leaning against the counter near me watching. "Let me finish this then I will be done for the day. Trying to get a head start while I can so I can spend time with you tomorrow. Know you have to leave again Monday."

"About that," Brantley said turning one of his biker rings around on his finger looking down at his boots. I stopped what I was doing to look at him as he met my eyes. "Why don't you go with me?"

"Yea okay.." I drawled rolling my eyes resuming my task. I heard a low growl making my eyes widen. "What, you are serious aren't you?"

"Umm... yes," he grumbled crossing his arms over his chest. I swore he was about to pout. I know there were thousands of fan girls that would drop what they were doing for that, but I had a business to run. "Let me show you around Nashville. You would have a blast baby. My year is just going to get busier."

"So is mine B," I sighed hating this. But we both had demands on our time. "I will be literally running around like a chicken with my head cut off from now until July. Valentine's is coming up. Then it's Easter, and dear lord at the weddings between now and then. I had an investor stop by the other day mentioning wanting to help me expand to Athens. Do you realize what that would mean for me? Stephanie and I are seriously looking into this. As much as I would love to go traipsing all over the country with you I can't always do it."

"A wedding cake is a wedding cake darlin," Brantley sighed making my eyes narrow at him. Ummm..not always at least to some people. He shuffled his feet starting to pace around my kitchen. I wasn't stupid man got itchy feet mentioning commitment. Why even though I know we were together the words boyfriend and girlfriend were rarely used. I had even made the comment to Sadie the other day that pretty sure him getting back on the road, promoting an album, and all the commitments I had were probably about to test us. "Why do people even wanna get married anyhow? Too many times it doesn't work out. Then what all you have is pictures you don't want. Overpaid for a dress and a cake. Nah, doesn't make sense."

"You don't want that?" I asked my jaw dropping a little as I sat the bag of icing in my hand down putting my hands on my hips. If my eyebrows went any further up my head they would be part of my hair. "Like ever?"

"And you do?" Brantley asked me with wide eyes turning pale. Well shit here we go. I shook my head in disbelief. "Suzie Q, you were just saying how busy you were a minute ago to pick up and go with me. So how can you expect to find time for that." I glared at him tamping down a growl. "What? You just said that."

"I know what I said!" I snapped seeing his eyes narrow back at me. "But yes, I do want that someday. Can't believe you don't!"

"Pardon me for my track record with women!" Brantley snapped back both of our voices getting louder. My heart was pounding. I was I no hurry, but still guess I was getting my answers on if we would ever be there. "But no, I'm not sure I would want that."

"Then," I snarled feeling tears bubble up in my eyes. "I guess we don't have anything else left to talk about."

"What the fuck do you mean Susanna Grace!" he yelled chest starting to heave as he stalked closer to me. I skirted him trying to focus back on what I needed to do. I had been right all along in some ways. He was just playing games with me. I could see myself with him down the road. Part of the reason I was contemplating expanding. With Steph and I partnering on it, I could free myself up to travel with him. But hell if I would tell him that now. "Explain right now."

"Don't you start barking orders at me!" I yelled back my hands shaking. I threw the icing bag down on the counter debating on throwing it at his stubborn head. "Take that tone with me and I will dump this whole cake on your head!"

"Like to see you try!" Brantley growled slamming his hands down on the counter as we faced off. "Are you saying you are done with us?"

"Define us!" I taunted back with a scoff rolling my eyes. I saw the door leading from the front open a crack as Stephanie stuck her head in. "The most we are is sleeping together I guess. Hell when you took me to see Jason a couple months ago I got introduced as Susanna. There was no girlfriend mentioned in that. Then lets not forget the reporter you made sure had stars in her eyes over you at the CMA's. Your commitment phobia is showing BG, might wanna tuck that shit back in."

"You never even said you wanted to go to the CMA's with me!" he yelled trying to walk closer to me but stopped as I raised a finger at him. "I would have loved for you to been on my arm."

"You didn't ask!" I seethed realizing it had bothered me more than I wanted to admit. I had buried it under being busy. "Thanks for making me feel like a hopeful idiot that you would when I found out Luke, who knew Sadie barely a week, asked, no begged her to go!"

"Didn't think this was high school," he grumbled rolling his eyes making me even madder. "And you were worried about the boy asking you to the dance Susanna. Thought we were older than that."

"Y'all," Stephanie snapped from the doorway shaking her head and looking back behind her. She pointed at the back door. "You two might wanna take it outside. Granny Hale and Nana Gilbert's Sunday school class just walked in. Even the ones who are in desperate need of hearing aids can read y'all loud and clear. This is not the place for a couple squabble."

"What couple," I snapped making her gasp. "All I seem to be is a fuck buddy." I heard a deep growl making me tremble for half a second. "But duly noted Steph. Brantley was just leaving."

"The fuck I was!" Brantley roared as Stephanie sighed shutting the door. Great, he was going to get both of us on the prayer list for our mouths alone. "We are not done darlin."

"Yes we are," I stated through clenched teeth keeping my emotions locked down. "I may not want those things right now, but I would one day and you are very adamant you don't. Let's not split hairs B. We had a good run. Had a lot of fun. But that's all that this has been." I forced myself to calmly pick up the bag of icing to finish the complicated flowers I was working on. I could make myself keep going. "You know where the door is Brantley."

"Susanna," Brantley said quietly as I focused on what I was doing trying to will myself to not cry. A hand landed on my shoulder making me shrug it off as I continued to not look at him. "Baby, you don't mean that. Maybe I answered that wrong..."

"We both know you always are up front and honest B," I said so softly I almost didn't hear myself. "Best to get this done now before someone gets hurt. I'll see you around. Think my jacket is at your house from the other day. Drop it off here next chance you get. Be safe on the road."

He stood there for a second looking at me in shock before turning to stomp out the back door slamming it behind him. It sounded like a gunshot making my mask slip as I slid down the counter dissolving into tears covering my mouth to muffle the sobs. I tried to remind myself it was for the best. The next morning I slipped into the pew beside Sadie flashing a quick smile at Ryleigh before slumping down. I had purposely bypassed Mama and Daddy both. Judging by the stares when I walked in, the overheard argument from yesterday had made its rounds. I was tempted to keep my sunglasses on even if it was cloudy outside just to hide the fact that I had spent the night eating ice cream, crying, and drinking wine. A soft hand landed on mine as I pulled my glasses off. I turned my head meetings Sadie's eyes.

"Oh Suz," she sighed squeezing it. "Are you okay? Mama called to tell me then I tried you but..."

"I didn't want to talk to anybody," I said quietly shaking my head. "It's done. Really is for the best Sadie. It really is."

"Luke said he was on his way to Nashville early when he called earlier," she murmured to me quietly. I bit my lip to keep from crying at the thought that he was that anxious to get away from me it seemed. "You need anything?"

"Just for the gossip to die down so I can get on with my life," I sighed shrugging my shoulders. "I really will be okay. Wasn't like we were serious anyways."

Before I get sent in the teepee...look at the year . save me!

Just Desserts We Don't Like

March 2014

Susanna's POV

I puffed out a sigh sitting in my office off the side of the kitchen at the bakery going over an order I was placing when Cheyenne knocked lightly pulling my attention. Okay, I really hadn't been focusing. More like moping. Maybe a little hiding. It had been like a three-ring circus around here ever since news that Brantley and I had broken up from whatever it was that we were doing. I mean, I was thankful for the business but damn people. That ass had gotten lucky because he'd been out of town since doing a radio tour promoting the upcoming album and taking care of things for the tour kicking off soon. Sure, leave me here to answer allllllllll the questions. To get allllllllll the wandering stares and whispers. I growled thinking about it making Cheyenne gasp as I finally lifted my head to meet her curious stare.

"What you need Cheyenne?" I asked with a tired grimace. A mischievous smile was on her hot pink lips. She jerked a thumb towards the swinging door leading out into the main floor.

"There is someone here to see you," she said with a chuckle. I felt my heart skip a beat mad at myself for the twinge of hope stirring in my chest. I pushed back from my chair smoothing a hand over my messy bun wiping at my face knowing there was more than likely flour there. I eased the door open stepping out biting my lip trying to keep a smile in. But when I focused on the man leaning against the counter smiling at me I almost wanted to cry. Deep brown ones in place of the piercing green ones I was hoping along with styled black hair.

Kenny Macon shot me a grin as I stepped closer trying to keep a groan in. Yes, I had secretly been hoping it was Brantley since his mama had dropped the gossip to my mama he was coming home for a week in the next few days. The starched dress shirt and slacks had me wishing for a tight black t-shirt and ripped jeans. I forced a bright smile on my face. We had been on a couple dates the last few weeks. Like ever since he heard things had ended with me and B, he had stepped up his game.

"Kenny," I said softly as his smile widened. Don't get me wrong he was handsome. A lawyer doing really well for himself, but I still saw the sixteen-year-old boy that had hung me out to dry. Mama said I needed to let past grudges go. Daddy on the other hand threatened to shoot him if he pulled that shit on me again. Mumbled something about taking care of him last time under his breath. I had no clue what he meant other than putting him through hell at football practice. "What brings you by?"

"Well," he said giving me a flirty smile that I forced myself to return. "I was wondering if you would be in the mood to take a ride into Athens later for some dinner. There is this amazing steakhouse I went to with a client the other day."

"Sure," I agreed with false cheeriness that I didn't feel. But what the hell. I had to move on didn't I. Kenny had seemed to change with age. "That sounds great."

"Okay Suz," Kenny said with a grin leaning over the counter to kiss my cheek. "I'll pick you up at seven thirty."

"Okay," I squeaked out as he walked away to keep a groan in. Didn't the damn man remember that I have to be up super early each morning. Guess not.

Brantley's POV

I wearily climbed out of my truck in Mama's driveway. It had been a long month that was for damn sure. I'd spent only a day home here and there for the last almost two months and it was starting to show. At least I had a week this time before needing to be back in Nashville for final tour rehearsals then it was on the road we went. Walking through the house I let the smell of her home cooking lead me. I spotted her at the stove cooking away praying I didn't have to wrestle my baby brother for the mac and cheese she was fixing. I pressed a kiss on the top of her soft blonde hair hugging her tight.

"Glad you are home son," Mama laughed turning to look up at me. A soft hand resting on my cheek before pointing at a chair. "Sit down baby. You look dead on your feet."

"I think I could sleep for a week," I sighed rubbing a hand over my face. "A few days in my own house will be good. Tired of the damn bus."

"Well you can relax then," she chuckled while stirring dishes making my mouth water. "Haven't missed too much while you were gone. Though I do believe Luke is spending more time here in Georgia than he has in Nashville. I passed him dropping Ryleigh off at school the other morning. He is nuts over those girls."

"I know," I muttered praying she didn't bring up Susanna. I'd done my best not to think about her or what went down before I left. Or that she was the reason why the couple of days I had been home I snuck in like a thief in the night to avoid her. "Had dinner with him last week while he was in town. They were all he could talk about and how ready he was to get back and see them. He seems really happy with Sadie. It shows big time."

"Hmm..." Mama drawled thoughtfully. My spine went ramrod straight knowing she was about to say something. A hand on one slim hip as the other shook a wooden spoon at me. I didn't have the energy to run away from her right now so I was praying she wouldn't beat me with it. "About like you were with a certain beautiful baker until you stuck your foot in your mouth. She was perfect for you son."

"And how pray tell do you know what was said Mama?" I grumbled raising an eyebrow. "Susanna and I were the ones having that conversation as I recall."

"Son," she snickered rolling her eyes. "You two were not exactly quiet when yelling and your Nana heard it word for word. Called me to fill me in and advised I ear tug you for her or wash your mouth out with soap. Your commitment issues just had to show didn't they."

"Mama," I whined earning me a glare. "I screwed up okay! That what you want me to admit! Maybe we could have had something great but now it's too late."

"Yep," Mama said with a chuckle making me feel worse than I already had been. Hell that was why I hadn't been home. The damn pillow on my bed still smelled like vanilla cupcakes. Actually rolled over reaching for her only to find I was alone. I missed her. I will admit that. So much that when Ben had climbed on the bus two weeks ago with the customary two dozen chocolate cupcakes, I had tossed a box out the window of the moving bus right in the middle of the interstate in Atlanta. PJ and Jesse had tackled me before I could do the same thing with second box. Ben had sat on me until they could hide them. "Probably is too late. She's been out on a couple dates with Kenny Macon recently. Sat with her at church last Sunday. Got a lot of admiring eyes from the woman's bible study group."

"Do...fucking...what?" I growled through clenched teeth feeling my hands ball into fists. That douche bag had taken her out. My blood boiled with rage in the blink of an eye. Bad enough he treated her like crap in high school. Something that I was not supposed to know anything about because I made a promise. But it was like he had been biding his time before he made a move. Like the fucker hoped we wouldn't work out. I'd noticed before she ended things he made a point to come in the bakery for coffee. Like the dipshit didn't own a coffee pot. "She went out with that asshole!"

"Unless you want to chew on a bar of soap," Mama hissed glaring at me. "You better watch your mouth Brantley Keith."

"Well it really is physically impossible to watch my mouth Mama," I grumbled back knowing I was being a smart ass. Said wooden spoon came flying at my head. I threw my hands up as I ducked. "Yes mam! I'm sorry. But it pisses me off okay!"

"So what?" Mama cackled giving me no sympathy at all. "You let her walk away and don't even try to lie saying you didn't. Jesus is watching son. Did you even bother to fight for her? No. You tucked tail and ran to Nashville. Go to M.O. isn't it baby boy. Break her heart before she can break yours?"

"My love life is not up for discussion," I growled back narrowing my eyes only to have her give me the same look in return.

"Too late B," she snickered rolling her eyes. "Been the talk of town for over a month. But you wouldn't know because you haven't been here more than a handful of hours. Left Susanna to be the one to deal with all the wondering looks and questioning eyes. Poor girl looks exhausted and well, between you and me, been hiding a few hangovers. I also would avoid Sadie if I was you. She's liable to painfully remove your balls. I would like grandchildren before I'm too old to enjoy them!"

The next afternoon I drove through town on my bike trying to get out of my own head with my blues. Hanging a right I decided it might not hurt to at least attempt to talk to Susanna. Maybe I could catch her leaving the bakery. She and I in a room full of sharp kitchen instruments probably wouldn't be a good idea. I pulled along the opposite side of the street parking, but by the time I had killed the engine reaching for the strap to undo my helmet, I noticed something that made me pause.

Inside the bakery, I spotted Kenny leaning against the counter talking to Susanna as she rearranged the cupcake display. The bastards lifted his hand up tucking a stray lock of auburn hair behind her ear making my heart twist as she flashed a smile at him. I remembered how silky her hair always felt and usually smelled like honeysuckle reminding me of spring. Fuck this. I didn't need to see that or for her to know I did. I started the engine hammering the gas to get out of town. I needed to shoot something before I exploded with anger and jealousy.

Luke's POV ( )

"You drink, I shoot," BG grumbles and drops a case of beer at my feet. Don't have to tell me twice. I crack open the first cold one leaning back into the chair while he lines up random shit to shoot. BG stalks back and forth looking as if he rather have Susanna's date from the other night lined up instead. The first shot rings out drowning out his misery he mutters beneath his breath. "Can't believe she went out with that punk," he shakes his head without ever looking over towards me.

"He didn't seem that bad of a guy," I shrug. BG jerks his head in my direction. I down the rest of the beer and quickly make my way over to line it up as a target.

"And how would you know, Luke?" BG stomps towards me before I can make it back to the chair. "You don't know that piece of shit. Susanna deserves better!" His eyes become filled with more rage while I try to hold back a laugh. "What's so fucking funny?"

"Nothin man. She had someone better," darting around him, I head back to my spot and grab another beer. The anger flowing through him is heard by every hard stomp into the ground. He shoots off every last target before dropping his head with a heavy sigh. "You know I'm right."

"Doesn't matter anymore," he slides his phone out of his pocket checking it with a familiar look I know all too well. He keeps a permanent scowl on his face. Too damn stubborn to be happy again.

BG resumes shooting while I continue knocking back the beer. A good buzz kicks in when I stand up to go line up another empty beer can. I thought I heard a slight chuckle from BG when I about busted my ass but when I turned around all I saw was his harden composure. Susanna and him need to pull their heads out their asses. Sadie said Susanna is just as bad except trying to hide the evidence of crying anytime Sadie walks into the bakery. Ryleigh asked where Uncle B was one day shortly after the split and Susanna hastily excused herself to the back of the bakery. That woman wears a transparent smile nowadays. Even on her date with Kenny Macon didn't make Susanna smile like BG can.

"Guess she's happy huh?" BG asks with a side glance. Jaw clenched tightly, he focuses back on reloading.

"You know man," I stumble my way over to him clamping a hand down on his rigid shoulder. "You need to get your girl back. She might or might not have worn a smile like the one you give her." BG shows a curious grin until I smile back at him making it disappear. He shrugs and moves past me. He raises the gun then lowers it glancing over at me. "That smile didn't reach her ears."

"Is that so," he says more to himself than me before turning back raising his gun again.

"So what are you going to do about it?" I feel my phone vibrate taking it out to see a text from Sadie. "I see my girlfriend just got off work," I let out a low whistle of the picture Sadie sends me to poke the bear some.

"Don't push it Luke," BG growls. His knuckles become white gripping the gun aimed at the empty beer can. Probably not the smartest to push him right now but hell if he shoots me at least I think he won't shoot to kill.

"Don't know what you mean," I stand up realizing driving isn't the best option right now. BG grumbles something about Susanna and Kenny kicking the rocks at his feet. "I'll wait for my girlfriend to come pick up my drunk ass. Maybe if you pulled your head out of your ass and talked to Susanna you can have your woman again."

Thank you for our favorite ass shaker's POV of what appears to be a very jealous BG. Question is....what's he gonna do about it?

Heavy Eyes, Tired Heart

L ate March 2014

Susanna's POV

My low heels clicked on the sidewalk as I wearily made my way across the church parking lot. Easter was next week, and I had been so dang busy my eyes were crossed. Things were moving forward with the investor, so Stephanie had been location scouting for us. I needed a week vacation just to sleep. I had blackmailed Steph to not tell mama about the cot I had in my office for naps since I was spending most nights at the bakery catching a few hours of sleep before running home to get a shower. Kenny had been preparing for a big case, so our little bit of dating had waned. Not that it really bothered me. That had been quickly going downhill in a hurry. I'd tried just couldn't make myself feel it.

I made my way in the church stopping to hug Granny Hale getting a pointed look in her sharp eyes that I strayed away from after kissing her cheek. I had just settled down into the pew beside Tiffany when Katie Benson turned around giving me a smirk. Closing my eyes, I silently prayed she would leave me alone. She had been the biggest bitch to me in high school. Made my life a living hell every chance she had gotten. Perfectly teased dark brown hair was idly flipped over her fake tan shoulders as an evil smile twisted on her lips. A look of fake sympathy in her eyes. Bitch was about as sympathetic as a spider is to a fly winding it into its web.

"How are you handling the news Susanna honey?" she drawled with fake sorrow. Tiffany laid a hand on my leg trying to keep me calm. Seems they all knew something I didn't.

"What news would that be Katie?" I asked through clenched teeth. The one day church was running late on starting. "I've been busy lately so no time for idle gossip. I have a business to run unlike some people who chase marriage for sport."

"Well seems you aren't the only one who has moved on from the previous relationship," Katie informed me with a smug smile. "Looks like BG has replaced you with the past. Or at least that is what I had heard. They were spotted...."

"Shut up Katie," I hissed not feeling this today. I couldn't hide how I really felt even though I wanted to. My heart literally felt like it was cracking. "I don't care what he does okay. I'm the one who ended things anyways."

"Oh you do care Susanna," Katie said with a snort rolling her heavily made up eyes. I pushed to my feet feeling my temper flare not caring that this wasn't the place. This bitch was pushing my buttons and relishing in it. I was about to give her what she wanted. A fist across her face right in the middle of the sanctuary. "You always had thing over him. I remember you drooling over him back in high school and not even in league with him. What ever would make you think you would be now? He's better off with her."

"You've got two seconds to hush it up before I make you," I snarled standing up. Katie pursed her lips at me with a quiet laugh thinking I wouldn't do it. I was about to prove her skanky ass wrong. I was in the middle of raising my arm to do just that when a firm grip wrapped around my left bicep yanking me out of the pew. I was whirled around and marched out the back doors hearing a flurry of whispers with each step. Well here went the gossip for the week. Feeling myself drug out into the spring morning, I yanked my arm out of the prison it was in snarling up at Brantley. "Get your damn hands off me."

"Oh I'm sorry," he grumbled crossing his arms over his chest returning my glare. The fire in those green eyes making my knees tremble. This was the first time we had been face to face since the day we spilt up. "Thought I was keeping you from catching an assault charge in the middle of the worship service."

"Was hearing all about your new girlfriend," I hissed pushing a hand into the middle of the gray t-shirt he was wearing making him rock back on his heels. I felt my eyes welling with tears that I couldn't tamp down due to exhaustion. Dammit. Not how I wanted things to go seeing him again. Preferred to be calm and aloof. Brantley's jaw clenched while he narrowed his eyes trying to step closer to me. God help me if even slipped an arm around me I would crumble into a bawling mess. "Or wait, guess if would be an old flame reignited!"

"Really?" he snapped with temper simmering under the surface. "You've been dating that jackass Kenny Macon lately or so I have heard. Had to hear it from my own damn mama Susanna. My....own...mama. Talking about being blindsided. Thought you were too busy."

"Thought you were too," I hissed before letting out a squeak when he towered over me. Gave me a good whiff of that cologne that made me weak in the knees. Dammit, I didn't need him to know that I missed him so much some days it hurt. Throwing my hands up, I glared at him in defiance. "You know what. I don't have to have this conversation with you! Just leave me alone."

"Oh yes we are," Brantley said trying to reach for my arm pulling me back. I noticed Sadie at the doors of the church trying to shew all the nosey old ladies back inside. I groaned feeling my face turn blood red. Well, business should be booming this week with them coming in for gossip. Bless her she was a great friend for trying. But it was like herding cows back to pasture after the gate had been opened. I slapped at the hand on my arm earning me a growl that stopped me in my tracks for half a second. Before I turned on my heel stalking away. "Get back here Susanna Grace! We are not done!"

My only response as a raised middle finger over my shoulder as I stalked off. Partially torn with wanting him to chase me and partially hoping he didn't. I shook it off climbing in my Jeep speeding off. Well, if I was going to skip church then I could work. The next afternoon, I watched Sadie make her way out of the bakery feeling even more weary from our conversation. I wished I could take her worry away. I aimed to do what I could to help. A flash of black caught the corner of my eye as I stepped to the back.

Surely not. I boxed up a couple orders before wiping my hands on my bright pink apron then pushed through the swinging door to let Josh know he could go ahead and go. I stopped in my tracks seeing Brantley there with his hands shoved in his pockets studying me. Shit. There was nowhere I could go hide either. I threw my shoulders back turning to look at Josh who was studying the pair of us with wide eyes. The questions were spinning in his mind for sure.

"Go ahead and go Josh," I sighed stepping closer to the counter. "I will see what BG here needs then close up. See you tomorrow." I turned back looking at Brantley. "What can I do for you?"

"Mama sent me after a dozen of your chocolate delight cookies that she said she ordered," he said resting his forearms on the display case studying me. I grabbed a box filling the order she had dropped by to pay for on her lunch break. Guess I'd wrongly assumed she would be the one coming back for it.

Josh squeezed my shoulder in support as he headed towards the front door. The bells jingled signaling his exit making me finally lift my head meeting those of the man observing me. I absently tucked a loose strand of hair out of my face. "You look exhausted Suzie Q."

"Busy, busy," I murmured shrugging my shoulders wishing he would just leave so I could have the possible coming breakdown in peace. "Well if that's...."

"I'm not back with Amber," Brantley said with a sigh studying me. I felt my eyes widen at his words. "That's what you had heard at church yesterday isn't it?"

"So what if it was," I grumbled feeling my insides flip. Why was he bringing this up? I glared at him. "Not like it is any of my business remember."

"I did see her yes," he said following me as I moved towards the register busying myself with closing out for the day. A hand on mine stilled me. I felt the contentment with that one touch soar through my veins. "Talked to her at my mailbox Saturday. At..my..mailbox Susanna. She was in town to see her mama. You get what that means right if I ran into her there. Means I talked to her and her husband both. Things aren't always what they seem darlin."

"Still doesn't change the fact it's none of my business," I snapped shoving the box of cookies at him pointing at the door. "You know your way out still I presume. I've got to close up."

"Fine," Brantley growled taking the box and stomping out. I collapsed against the counter covering my face with my hands feeling even lower than I did once I heard his motorcycle roar to life outside. God, was I destined for this the rest of our lives. Fucking curse of living in a small town. Later on, I had lost track of what time it was. My eyes burned with shed tears and forcing myself to keep them open as I pulled yet another tray of sugar cookies in the shape of eggs out to transfer to a cooling rack. They would be ready for Steph or I to decorate tomorrow.

One more batch and I would make myself get a couple hours in my office before going home to shower. Mama was gonna catch on to what I was up to before I knew it. I felt myself nodding standing straight up when a voice sounded behind me. I screamed whirling around tripping over my bare feet. Arms wrapped around my waist pulling me up right. The smell of cologne, wind, and cigarettes teased my nose making me gasp.

"What are you doing here?" I sniffled swaying on my feet. I couldn't push away from him right now even if I wanted to. "It's like two in the morning."

"Couldn't sleep," Brantley answered gruffly. Long fingers smoothed along my spine I knew out of habit. But it was quickly doing what it always did and that was making my eyes heavier than they already were with each stroke. "Went for a drive to clear my head. Saw your Jeep in the lot and the light on back here. Remembered where the spare key was." He slipped a hand under my chin making me look up at him. "Baking and crying is not a good combination you've told me before. You've been doing both sweetheart."

"Tears are because I'm overwhelmed and busy," I grumbled knowing I wasn't even telling myself the whole truth. I missed the man staring down at me like a more than I even wanted to admit to myself. Why the hell did we both have to be so stubborn. Mama told me it was a trait I inherited from Daddy she'd been determined to beat out of me when I was younger. I went to push away from him only to have the arms holding me band tighter. "I'll get some rest when I finish this batch."

"Nope," Brantley warned lowly. The low tone of his voice had the hairs on the back of my neck stand up. Wasn't the only thing on my body that stood up at the rough timber. Damn traitorous nipples. "You are dead on your feet Suzie Q." His eyes narrowed to something behind him before a low growl rumbled through his chest. I ducked my shoulders looking down at my feet knowing exactly what he had seen through the door of my office. He puffed out a deep sigh. "Dammit Susanna. You been sleeping here?"

"Trying to get Easter orders done," I said quietly. "That and well just..it's that..."

"Yea," he said softly all the admonishment out of his voice. "I know what you mean. Look, go lay down. I'll put this stuff up. Cut the ovens off." I opened my mouth to argue only to be turned around pushed towards my office. I walked in there on blind feet laying down curling up in a ball. This is about the only time I could sleep without my mind wandering. Wondering if I took things out of context. Was I the cause of things ending? Maybe.... the lights in the kitchen switched off along with the ones in my office. I braced myself for the back door shutting but instead I heard quiet footsteps before the door to my office closed.

The edge of the cot dipped after the thud of boots sounded on the floor. My eyes burned with tears in the darkness feeling my tired body lifted as Brantley rolled me over to practically stretch out across him. My head nestled in the crook of his next unable to keep in the contented sigh. All the fight to stay awake seeped away with each trace of his fingers along the back of my t-shirt. A feather light kiss was pressed to the center of my forehead. "Get some sleep Suzie Q."

"Mmmkay," I mumbled holding onto the edge of his shirt fisted in my hand for dear life. This is what I had been needing just couldn't admit it. I quit fighting sleep relishing in being in his arms again even if it was just for this brief time. I could hold this memory tight with the rest of them to help me get through things. No matter how much I missed him, still didn't change the fact he didn't seem to want the same things I did eventually. Part of me hope he missed me just as much. Then the other part was afraid to find out that he didn't. The dredges of exhaustion and the warm body under mine pulled me under giving me what I needed right now. The rest would be whatever it would be.

Why oh why do they fight it???? Maybe, just maybe they will come around. Stay tuned to find out. ... think Miss Sadie may have a trick up her sleeve to help??

No Choice Given: Part I

Stephanie's POV

I clenched my jaw hearing the muffled conversation near the register. I was about to yank my cousin by the hair of her head all the way from Maysville to Nashville if that is what it took to get her out of her funk. Putting my hands on my hips, I pushed the swinging door open while Susanna brushed by me. I pretended for what felt like the millionth time that I didn't see the tears in her eyes. Swear that man brought out the stubbornness in her.

I rounded the counter catching up with Sadie. Between her and Tiffany someone had to have a plan of what we could do. I got even with her as we reached the door. I glanced behind me then pointed out to the sidewalk with Sadie falling in step with me. I took a quick glance around noting we seemed to be alone so there was no chance of the gossip chain hearing this.

"She's fucking miserable," I grumbled shaking my head as Sadie sighed nodding in agreement. If I wasn't so worried about Susanna I would probably call Sadie out on being miserable without Luke even though she was hiding it better. I threw my hands up in frustration. "Please tell me you got some ideas of what we can do. I could have sworn right before Easter something was changing when I came in to wake Susanna up because she was crashing here." Sadie let out a huff of annoyance. I knew exactly how she felt. "Found BG sneaking out the back to his truck. I couldn't even yell at him for toying with her because I knew she had finally gotten some sleep. He looked just a miserable as she is."

"Hmmm..." Sadie said pursing her lips then it was like a lightbulb went off behind her blue eyes. She gave me a wink. "Let me make a few calls. I may have an idea."

A few days later my phone lit up with a text from Sadie. Susanna notices the name but is so zoned out from her thoughts that it doesn't register for her. I grin doing a bit of a happy dance at what Sadie has up her sleeve. I answer her back before following Susanna into the kitchen. Bypassing her, I walk into the office grabbing her purse then turned to thread my arm through hers. Blazing amber eyes glare at me as I drag her towards the door. Literally could hear her feet digging into the floor.

"What the hell Steph?" Susanna snarled as I manhandled her out the back door pointing at her Jeep. I grinned batting my eyes at her. I swear if she wasn't so tired I would be getting a fist to the face. She tried to sidestep me going back inside but I flung myself against the door shaking my head. "Move! I've got a cake to finish!"

"Nope," I chuckled barring her way as she tried to dodge around me. She let out frustrated growl glaring at me stomping her foot. Well wasn't that cute. "Get out of here for a little while. This place will not fall in if you aren't here. I made you an appointment at Janie's to get your nails done. Maybe let her get ahold of your hair while you are there. Pamper yourself woman! You work hard. I will hold down the fort. Love you!"

Susanna let out a defeated sigh before giving in. I made sure she had gotten out of eyesight before I darted back inside running to the front to lock the door flipping the sign stating be back soon. I ran out the back shutting the door up heading to my car flying over to Susanna's. It's a good thing I knew most of the deputy's were on the other side of town or I would be baking extra cupcakes to bribe my way out of a ticket as I turn into Susanna's driveway on two wheels. Just to be an ass, I waved at the preacher's wife who was watching me curiously. This is why I live out in the country. No one around to keep up with the comings and goings from my house. I blushed thinking about the recent visitor knowing Susanna would give me hell for it. Why I had kept it quiet from her.

Glancing at my watch, I hurry through Susanna's house to her room. Flinging open her closet, I stand on tiptoe grabbing the first duffle bag I see with an evil chuckle. Oh if she just knew what we were up to. I grab the shorts I am looking for along with a few other random outfits. These were a must because they were cut off just right and showed off her tan legs. Don't need too many clothes though. Won't need it if all goes to plan. And I have absolute faith all it's going to take is this little, teeny, tiny push. I'm skipping out of the bathroom whistling when I stop in my tracks at Sadie leaning in the doorway laughing. I throw the packed bag at her with a snicker.

"Jesus Steph," she said with a gasp. If I didn't know better, I think she was a little excited for this trip too. "Did you pack her anything at all?" Sadie shook the bag making my grin widen. "Was expecting heavier."

"Meh," I said with an evil grin grabbing Susanna's charger off her night-stand. I noted the black hat draped from the lamp making my grin widen. Mhmmm wonder why she kept that close. "Not like she is gonna be in need of too much more than a toothbrush, deodorant, and a smile."

"She needs this so damn bad," Sadie sighed as we made our way to the door. "Afraid she is gonna bake herself to death. Even with the adding of the new location. She told me the chief baker there was amazing with cupcakes. But getting out of town is what she needs."

"She does," I agreed locking the house back up. "I've never seen her like this. So, any issues with getting the stuff? Know it had to be tough talking to Luke."

"We've been talking some," Sadie said slipping her sunglasses on with a blush. Talking huh. Wonder what the boyfriend thought about that. She needed to kick that dick face to the curb. He would show his true colors in time no doubt. "But I have all we need for this road trip."

"My question is," I drawled shaking my head. "what does Ryan say about this little trip?"

"Not a damn thing," Sadie snapped back shaking her finger at me. Ah, so it was like that huh. "He knows that Ryleigh is at my parents for the weekend. Told him I was getting Susanna out of town to cheer her up. He is on a need to know basis and that is all he needs to know!"

"Well yes mam," I grinned shaking my head. "Well let's head back. Susanna will be done with her manicure before we know it. Kicked her out earlier saying she needed some pampering. There will be only so long that Janie will be able to hold her captive for me."

An hour later, I was helping a customer when I heard the back door close. I motioned at Sadie, who was sitting a table sipping her coffee that Susanna was back. She jumped up following me to the back. Susanna absently humming to herself looking for an apron. If I didn't know better the tune was "If You Want A Bad Boy". Oh, if she only knew what I knew that a little birdie had told me about some of the songs on this newest album that dropped a few weeks ago. Her auburn hair was down with what looked like a fresh trim and newly manicured nails. Hearing the door close, her head jerked up seeing Sadie and I facing her.

"Hey," she said forcing a smile on her face. "I'm back Steph if you want to go relax for the day." I shook my head no making her pause mid tie of her apron frowning. "Seriously I've got this. You go hang out. Sadie, wanna see if Ryleigh wants to come chill with me and bake while you do something with Ryan. I'd be happy with her company."

"She's at Mama and Daddy's," Sadie said with an evil smile as we both flanked Susanna. "You and I have plans actually."

"Umm...." Susanna said confusion washing over her features. "I don't...."

"That's because it's a surprise," I chuckled when we both grabbed an arm. Heels immediately dug in on us. But no way she could fight both of us. What she didn't know was I had Kolby on standby just in case we needed a man to forcefully load her in Sadie's car. "You two are taking a road trip. I have the bakeries in hand. Aunt Connie is working for me in the morning. We got you covered Suz. Please go have some fun."

"I can't!" she yelped with a tinge of fear at having to leave the one thing that had kept her busy over the last few months. "I have..."

"Two seconds to get in the damn car so we can get on the road," Sadie growled pointing her finger. Even I winced because the mom voice had come out. "Your bag is packed. If you don't fight me I may fill you in on what the plans for the weekend are for. Fight me and I will ear tug you to the car kicking and screaming. It's your choice."

"Fine," Susanna hissed yanking her arms free throwing the apron back at me as I laughed. "I'll go. But dammit when I am behind next week and y'all are bitching about me overworking again y'all only have yourselves to blame!"

"Have fun Suzie Q!" I teased as she climbed in slamming the door. I gave Sadie a wink. "Keep me posted on how things go."

"Of course," Sadie laughed walking to her car with a sway of her hips and swinging ponytail. I had a feeling that woman had an agenda of her own while they were in Nashville. Bet she came back smiling bigger too.

Well, well, well. They've done some scheming. Sadie made some calls to a certain ass shaker that is covered in Crash My Party. Wonder what Susanna while say once she finds out there destination????? Stay tuned....

No Choice Given: Part II

Walking down the street from our hotel, I tugged my shorts down one more time glaring over at a snickering Sadie. Should have known better than to let Steph pack my bag. Well, not like I had known I was taking a trip. Why the hell she packed me so little I dunno. Already told Sadie we were going shopping tomorrow before we did anything else in Nashville. Evil woman wouldn't even tell me what concert we were going to. Only my dear sweet cousin or Tiff would find the skimpiest shirt and shorts that I own! The chiffon hunter green halter top was at least light weight and comfortable. Really did go well with my brown cowboy boots and cut off shorts. I looked like half the college coeds mingling around Nashville.

"Hurry up," Sadie said motioning for me to walk faster. Her brunette curls bouncing with each step like a woman on a mission. Thought we were up here to relax. "We are gonna be late."

"Which you still won't tell me what for!" I snapped knowing I was acting like a two-year-old. They were right. I did need a break even if I didn't want to admit it. Getting out of town away from the memories I was slowly drowning in was a welcome change. It was even worse if I knew Brantley was home. We followed a group of chattering girls while Sadie dug two passes out of her shorts pocket draping one around my neck before I could read it. I knew we were going to a concert and something told me she'd gotten Luke to hook her up. Hope for her sake we were seeing him because even though she hid it, I knew she missed him.

Threading her arm through mine I grinned over at her as we made our way to a white tent. Curiosity finally got to me so I looked down at the pass to see what it said only to have a picture of Brantley staring back at me. Shit! No! I growled lowly in my throat making Sadie throw her head back laughing. "I'm going to fucking kill you Sadie. I can't do this."

"Ohhhh yes you can," she teased. She at least had us in the back of the room. I could hear the excited screams when a moment later Jesse walked on the small stage with a guitar followed not even two seconds later by Brantley. The black hat backwards. White tank top with a pair of ripped black jeans. I felt my heart pounding out of my chest torn with the desire to get the hell out of there before I was spotted. He more than likely would be pissed that I was there. Sadie reached out squeezing my arm leaning in to whisper in my ear as they started to play. "No, he doesn't know you are here. Luke got Kerri to handle the passes and tickets for the show. It's up to you in a way if you see him."

"But it wouldn't hurt either of you," a voice said from beside me making me jump. I turned to see Ben leaning against the wall near us giving me a smirk. "He misses you Suzie Q. Won't say it but he does."

"Doesn't matter," I murmured turning my attention back to the man at the front of the room as he started answering fan question. The flirty smile to the blonde in the front that yes he was single made my chest ache. But I couldn't get upset. I had given up the right months ago. Biting my lip, I looked at my booted feet feeling Ben wrap an arm around my shoulders while Sadie sighed. Guess they all had been in on this scheme. Lifting my head, a gasp lodged in my throat when I locked eyes with the green ones staring intently to the back of the room. They widened seeing me before he let professional cool take over. Unable to take it, I pushed away from Ben ducking out of the tent with he and Sadie both trailing me. I whirled around outside blinking my eyes to fight against the tears. "I can't y'all please don't make me. Bad enough now that he knows I am here."

"That's a good thing!" Sadie snapped growling at me. "Stop being a chicken shit walking away from the damn man. You need him."

"I can take you back with me," Ben told me gently as he jerked his head towards the buses. "Find somewhere quiet for you two to talk. You need to Suzie Q. It's past time and here you don't have the bakery to hide behind."

"No," I hissed turning on my booted foot stalking away from them pointing at the arena. "All I am going to do right now I go find me a drink!"

Later the beers I had chugged earlier were swirling through my veins as Sadie pushed me closer to the stage. I had no choice she had already ear tugged me into the pit with an evil smile determined for me not to hide. I wanted the concrete floor to open up swallowing me away. Unable to help myself I watched Brantley standing on the stage with rapt attention. Long fingers playing his guitar that made me bite my lip even from this distance.

Rough timber of his voice live doing unspeakable things to my hormones. Been a long time since I had seen him play and was well worth it. From the older songs that I'd heard for years to the newest ones from the latest album I watched unable to not sway my hips a little to the music. A group of college girls moved prompting Sadie to shove me towards the open space by the stage filling the hole. A guitar rift made my eyes widen as Brantley passed his guitar off before grabbing his mic starting the song off walking down the stage.

Suddenly as he started to sing, ironically the song that was my secret favorite off the new album, he was standing above us and closer than I'd been to him in two months. Looking down his eyes locked with mine stilling me in place while all the other women around me screamed shoving to get closer. A long ringed finger crooked at me when I felt a forceful shove from Sadie putting me against the railing as Brantley leaned down holding a hand out for me. I gasped feeling myself tugged upwards as I landed onstage feeling instantly wobbly on my booted feet as reality set in.

"If you want a bad boy," Brantley sang looking down into my eyes with a wink as I turned a million shades of red. He played it up like I was just some random girl he pulled on stage making we wonder if this was a nightly thing. But the gentle hand resting on my bare arm teased my senses with the hidden stroke of his thumb. Who knew the inside curve of my elbow was so sensitive? "Then baby you got it. Got a bad toy sittin in the parking lot." Once the song was over he held an arm out to the crowd with a wink before stepping closer giving me a devilish smile that I knew all too well that he was damn certain made me weak in the knees. He leaned down to whisper in my ear guiding me to the edge of the stage. Felt his chest against my arm no doubt inhaling deeply because he swore I always smelled like vanilla cupcakes. "Go find PJ to help you to the back. I'll be offstage soon."

My feet touched the ground with the help of the closest security guy. I could feel the death glares from at least fifty fan girls near us as Sadie smirked at me. She threw an arm around my shoulders but reality of what had just happened set in. Why would he want me back there? Was I expected to be the fling for the night while he was in town? I suddenly felt all the beer I drank trying to come back up so I took off running pushing through the crowd with Sadie hot on my heels. She grasped my arm spinning me around.

"What the hell Susanna?" she asked studying me with concern. "What is wrong? What did he tell you?"

"Wants me to meet him back stage," I answered with a trembling voice shaking my head. "I can't Sadie."

"Yes you can," she challenged narrowing her eyes at me. I felt tears welling as she snarled at me. "It's the least you owe that damn man."

"No!" I yelped turning to stalk away. I got to the edge of the railing that separated the pit from the rest of the crowd as I looked back to see if she was following me. Since I wasn't looking I smacked into a hard chest the only then stopping me from busting my ass was a big hand gripping my elbow. I looked up with a squeak hearing a deep chuckle.

"Well hello cupcake," PJ said with a snicker as Sadie stepped even with me. "Been a while. Ready to go?"

"No, I am not!" I snapped just as Sadie answered, "Oh yes she is!"

"Honey," he laughed tightening his grip on my arm. "You act like you have a choice in all this. We both know that if you don't come with me he will tear Nashville apart looking for you."

Before I could protest, PJ took matters into his own hands just as Brantley wrapped up singing "Take It Outside". He tossed me over his broad shoulder. Sadie stood up on her tiptoes giving me a smacking kiss on the cheek.

"Have fun girlie!" she cackled pulling her phone out of her pocket snapping a picture. No doubt to add to the video she had filmed as well. "Be bad for me!"

"Dammit PJ!" I yelled as he turned with a wave to Sadie pushing through the crowd reaching the side of the stage. "Let me go!"

Hmmmmm.....wonder what will happen next. Seems like he's not bothered at all to see her. Maybe unload that foot from his mouth finally??? To get the details from the planning and the roadtrip up to Nashville check out Crash My Party

Special Delivery Boss....

B rantley's POV

Taking the bottle of water the roadie handed me, I hurried down the hall to the dressing room still a little in disbelief. Susanna was here tonight. I had been floored looking back during VIP seeing her standing in between Ben and Sadie. God, she looked so damn beautiful. Nervous as hell too. I'd noted she looked a bit more relaxed with a drink in her hand until Sadie shoved her towards the stage. I don't know how they got her here but was thankful they had. Last thing I think she expected was for me to pull her onstage tonight. Honestly had taken everything I had not to grab her and kiss her right then and there. Oh the way those cheeks had flushed when I was singing to her earlier. A song that she had been some inspiration in no less.

Pushing open the door, my face fell slightly not seeing Susanna standing there waiting on me. I thought for sure she would be. I growled throwing the bottle of water across the room running a hand over my head in aggravation. I patted my pockets to pull out a cigarette realizing I had left my pack on the bus. Dammit! That was it, I was calling Luke when I wrapped up meet and greet for Sadie's number so I could find Susanna. I doubted she would answer my calls.

Been a thought warring through my mind for months as my finger would hover over her contact but too afraid to call. I had screwed up so bad when it came to her. I just wanted to make it right. Wanted her back. Thought throwing myself into work and touring was the solution to keep my mind off her. I was in the middle of going for broke texting Luke for Sadie's number when the door flew open. I whirled around seeing PJ stroll in grinning with five foot of pissed off woman over his shoulder. I heard Susanna growl yelling at him.

"I swear Cupcake if you hit me one more time....Think I found something you misplaced Boss," he chuckled. She stopped mid rant when she heard me laugh. "Where do you want me to put her?"

"On my damn feet for starters!" Susanna hissed landing a fist in the middle of his back making him wince. "Now!"

"You heard the lady," I chuckled as PJ flipped her off his shoulder. Susanna whirled around seeing me and gulped. I got a wink as he silently backed out the door closing it behind him. I couldn't say anything as we looked at each other. There was so much I wanted to say that I wasn't sure I'd be able to get it all out right. I silently prayed I didn't stick my foot in my mouth again. "It's good to see you darlin."

"Sadie..umm..she.." she said looking down at her feet pulling her bottom lip between her teeth nibbling on it in doubt. "Kind of a ......"

"You know what," I murmured shaking my head. "I don't care why just as long as you are here." Striding forward, Susanna's head jerked up as I reached her burying my fingers into her silky hair pulling her face to mine. "Fuck, I've missed you."

Sealing my lips on hers, I felt slim hands grip the front of my tank top yanking me closer. A low whimper bubbled up from her throat as her body melted against mine. Felt my world turn right just with a kiss from her. Everything I hadn't wanted to admit I missed. Too stubborn to shake the past off and focus in on what I had. Susanna pulled her head back looking up at me through her lashes.

"I've missed you too," she whispered softly. Fingers toying with the necklaces around my neck biting her lip. A quiet sigh came with the shake of her head. "It's also a mistake that I am here too. We are just going to do the same song and dance. Play the games we had been. I can't put myself through that again Brantley. I don't have the time to pick up the pieces of a broken heart again. Yes, there I said it. Ending things with you did break my heart! I can't do it again."

"No more games," I murmured shaking my head her eyes widened in shock. Amber colored pools that I had missed blinking open sleepily to stare at me. Had haunted me seeing the light out of them when I would be home. I had been a miserable asshole without her. Saying words I should have said months ago instead of being stubborn. "No more bullshit baby girl. What we have is so real and I am sorry for not seeing that. For not opening myself up to the possibility of it. You were right to do what you did. But I'm all in Susanna."

"No," she whimpered yanking her head from my hands tears slipping down her cheeks. She covered her mouth backing away from me. "I need to go find Sadie. I can't do this B. I honestly can't trust the fact you aren't saying this just to get what you want. That is a girl for the night. The convenient hookup you honestly made me feel like. I just can't...."

"Susanna, wait," I pleaded as she stalked to the door. Slumped shoulders faced me. "Please don't go."

"I've got to," Susanna murmured looking over her shoulder at me. The pain in her eyes cutting me to the quick "It's only worse if I don't. I will see you around town B."

Hearing the sound of her hand trying to turn the door knob snapped me to the reality she was leaving. I couldn't let her walk out of my life again.

"Don't go, please?" I asked one more time. The door cracked making what I had been hiding for months come out. "Dammit Susanna, I love you!"

"What did you just say to me?" she gasped whirling around. I made my feet move raising a hand above her shutting the door with a quiet snick. Could hear both our hearts pounding as a sob slipped past her lips. Her balled up fist hit my chest lightly as she shook her head in disbelief. "Don't you dare toy with me Brantley Keith. It's not funny."

"Do I look like I am joking Susanna Grace?" I asked lowering my hand to lift her chin up while wrapping my free arm around her waist pulling her to me. I brushed a stray tear off her cheek caressing it softly. Resting my forehead against hers, I let out a shaky breath. "I'm not playing around. I do love you. I should have spoken up sooner. Quit hiding behind my doubts months ago. I love you and I am all in for whatever comes our way."

"Really?" Susanna sniffled making a smile tug at my lips. "You mean it? You really do?"

"Feel that?" I asked lifting her hand up to rest over my heart. "That is all yours. Has been for quite a while now. If you aren't on that same page I..."

"I do," she murmured pushing up on her tiptoes kissing me deeply. "I do love you. Hadn't wanted to admit it to myself either."

"You think of walking away from me again," I chuckled pressing her against the door letting my hands trace along her body. "You are gonna have a fight on your hands." A sharp knock at the door stopped me in the middle of lowering my head back to hers. "Dammit, I really wish I didn't have meet and greets so I could take this a lot further."

"Go do what you have to," Susanna laughed pushing me back with a wink. "I'm not going anywhere."

"Damn right you aren't," I grinned lacing my fingers with hers lifting our joined hands up to brush a kiss along her knuckles. "Come on you're going with me. Keep the fan girls off what is yours."

Ahhhh look at him....he pulled his foot out of his mouth!!!! Seems there may be some making up to do. didn't you mention handcuffs?

Takin This Leap of Faith

S usanna's POV

Even though it was late, the sidewalk of the street heading to my hotel was still busy. Looking down at the fingers laced with mine I was tempted to pinch myself to see if I was dreaming. Had tonight really happened? Had Brantley really pulled me on stage in front of thousands of people while singing to me? This wasn't part of my small-town life. Not by a long shot. My hand lifted making my heart race as lips brushed gently along my knuckles feeling a chuckle as I blushed. But the words spoken earlier, those, those were now very much a part of my real life. I heard boots scrape on the sidewalk before I was turned my back hitting the wall of the building behind us. Fingers cupped my chin tipping my head up to make me look at him.

"What's going through that pretty little head of yours baby?" he asked his green eyes brimming with concern. Slight traces of worry there too. "Not having second...."

"Nooooo..."I said shaking my head giving him a bright smile. "No second thoughts at all. Guess the entirety of the situation is hitting me maybe. Things are a little different now."

"Ummm...I don't follow," Brantley said puzzled. "Other than telling you how I feel and not keeping my guard up what has changed?"

"We never defined what was between us last time either," I reminded him with a wince. This probably wasn't the best time to bring up past doubts between us. He shrugged knowing I was right before wrapping his arms around me pressing closer. I swallowed down a whimper at the devilment in his seductive eyes. Lips twisting up in a smirk that he knew damn well would make the panties I was wearing drop.

"Mine," he murmured leaning down biting my bottom lip with a dark chuckle. "Think I reminded about five teenage girls that were glaring at you tonight that I was very much off the market. Guess I should have kissed you onstage tonight like I really wanted to. I understand being with me comes with a very public side to things at times. But that's only part of the time. The rest of the time it will be dealing with being infamous in our small town. That right there gives me more worry than what fan girls or gossip columnists will say. I don't care truthfully as long as it doesn't start to effect you baby. I love you and that is all that matters."

"That still gets me," I admitted feeling my cheeks heat up while I wrapped my arms around his neck. "I don't ever want to stop hearing it."

"Well," Brantley murmured brushing his lips against mine while squeezing my hips. "Why don't we get your stuff because I am confident I have a few moves to back up the words baby girl."

"Mmm..."I teased pushing him back sliding my arm around his waist as we started walking again. The hotel within our sights. "Keep talking outlaw. I may be in desperate need of those moves."

"Tease," he hissed sliding a big hand into my back short pocket squeezing. "Think Sadie will be pissed if you took the bus back to Georgia with me Sunday? I was staying until then to do a song writing session, but Rhett cancelled on me. Maybe take you out to dinner somewhere tomorrow night?"

"I'm sure she will be fine," I snickered as we walked across the lobby. We stepped into the open elevator as I pushed the button for the floor. "She cooked up this whole scheme with Stephanie. Had some help from Luke as well. Think this was her plan was to drive home alone all along."

"I owe that woman a bottle of her favorite wine and a night babysitting Ryleigh," Brantley laughed as I pulled out my key card pointing down the hall. I couldn't help but laugh too. He was right. We both did. "She gave us both the push we needed."

"She did," I giggled trying to unlock the door as my hair was brushed away from my neck. Lips and teeth teasing along the sensitive curve made me shiver and moan. I leaned back pressing my body into his craving that connection I had been missing. Warm hands teasing at the hem of my shirt. With shaking hands, I finally got the door open sending us both tumbling into the room laughing like a pair of teenagers. I paused looking around not finding Sadie's bag or anything here. I gasped. "Where the hell is she?"

"I have a few guesses," Brantley murmured scraping his teeth across the delicate shell of my ear causing a tremble through my body. "Maybe she's taking her own advice and went to see Luke."

"Maybe," I moaned softly. A glint on the bed caught my eyes making them narrow. "What the...."

"Damn, I love that woman," he laughed slipping his arms from around me stepping closer. He picked the object turning to me with the handcuffs dangling from his finger with a sultry smile on his lips when I gasped. "Whatever will we do with these baby? Wanna put them to a test?"

"Ummm..." I whimpered watching him with wide eyes kick his boots off padding back over to me. I could feel the heat from his eyes searing through me. Panties up in flames....check.

"Or," he whispered slipping his hat off laying it on the nightstand along with the handcuffs. Fingers laced with mine pulling me towards the king-sized bed that had looked so soft earlier. Turning me gently, he pushed me back on the bed reaching down to tug my boots off for me. Fire simmered in his eyes while he teased rough hands along the smooth skin of my legs leaning down to kiss me deeply. Brantley broke the kiss staring in my eyes cupping my cheek. "I love you Susanna. Sorry it took me so long to realize it baby."

"I love you too," I whispered feeling the good tears well in my eyes. Pressing my hands to his cheeks I pulled his face to mine. "Show me."

Ask and you shall receive for sure. If anyone had told me things could be different once all walls were down in the past I would have told them they were crazy. As content exhaustion pulled me under as dawn creeped through the blinds, I wished I had spoken the words much sooner. But they were out there now and no taking them back from either of us.

Brantley's POV

Rolling to my side, I watched Susanna's smooth back ripple as she stretched. Auburn hair draped over her shoulder messily no doubt from having my hands buried in it more than from sleep. Sleep had not been of a high priority last night. A deep chuckle slipped past my lips watching her lift up her wrist rubbing it slightly making my dick ache at the memories. I so owed Sadie more than she knew. Those handcuffs had been a pure stroke of genius. Fingers snapping pulled me from my devilish thoughts of tackling Susanna for a repeat. I looked up grinning at her noticing the blush on her tan skin.

"You could quit looking so smug," she murmured turning around to look at me. A yelp sounded out as I yanked her down across my chest wrapping my arms around her. I felt lighter than I had in a long time. But I knew the craving of having her skin against mine would never ease. I shook my head pulling her down to capture her swollen lips with mine. Lost myself in the feel of her lips on mine. I'd kick my own ass if I was stupid enough to let her go again. Susanna broke the kiss pushing her hands on my chest looking down at me. She pursed her lips at me teasing a smile along mine. "I probably should call Susanna to let her know her plan worked."

"I got this," I chuckled tucking her into my side as I reached for my phone typing out a quick text to Luke. Trusted the feeling in my gut that Sadie was right there with him. Hoped they had worked things out. Know he had been as miserable as I had been. I practically could hear his laugh as I laid my phone back down turning to roll Susanna beneath me. Slim legs wrapped around my waist molding my body to hers. I could see the mischievousness twinkling in her eyes. "Now, where were we?"

Early Monday afternoon, I typed back a text to Luke that I would go by and double check Sadie's car for him once she made it home later. Knew it was just an excuse to assure him she made it back to Georgia fine. I'd had a quick meeting with Scott before we left Sunday. Susanna had opted to just wait for me on the bus instead of tagging along. I had climbed back on finding things quiet as we rolled out of Nashville. Walking into my room at the back, a chuckle had slipped out seeing Susanna curled up sleeping peacefully with Sylo, the puppy I had gotten after we split up, snoring at her hip.

Those two had fallen in love at first sight. Something had me betting his touring days would revolve around going with me or staying with her now. I'd bumped his black and white head when I laid down on her other side startling him awake. Teeth had gripped my hand gently moving it off

Susanna making my eyes widen as Sylo laid his head in the place of it. Okay, jealous dog trying to take over my girlfriend had been duly noted.

My boots echoed over the black and white tile floor of the bakery making me lift my head from my phone looking around. I swore all conversation from the ladies' choir sitting at a couple tables in the back halted as they all focused on me. I heard a quiet laugh from Stephanie standing behind the counter with a broad grin. I rolled my eyes at her then grinned seeing Susanna walk from the back wiping at her cheek totally missing the flour there. Sometimes I swore she was coated in it. A shy smile teased at her lips as I walked closer.

To my gruntled dismay, she had nimbly rolled out of bed at the crack of dawn this morning leaving me grumbling as she got ready for work. But I knew her having a business to run was part of it. Crooking a finger at her, Susanna laughed shaking her head bracing her hands on the counter leaning over it. I cupped the back of her head leaning down capturing her lips with mine. Gasps sounded through out the room as I deepened it hearing a quiet whimper from Susanna. Stephanie let out a big laugh clapping her hands. Yep, that would give the old ladies of town something to chew on for the week. I had my girl back so I couldn't care less right now.

Well they are back on again. Could be some adventures ahead. Stay tuned here and in Crash My Party to find out!

Adventures In Babysitting
And Beyond

S eptember 2014

Susanna's POV

I let out a laugh shoving a worried Sadie out of my front door. I heard a crash making me look over my shoulder into my living room with a wince. A giggling Ryleigh along with a growling Sylo currently had Brantley pinned to the floor doing their level best to keep him down. I hugged Sadie one more time pushing her into Luke's waiting arms as he headed to the truck with her. I shut the door leaning back against it a smile twisting at my lips at the scene before me. Ryleigh's giggles really were contagious as the infectious smile on her face. When Luke had mentioned wanting to take Sadie on a surprise trip for her birthday, we had jumped on the chance to keep Ryleigh. She was usually in the bakery at least once a week after school helping me or Stephanie with orders. If B was home she tagged along with him if he wasn't busy when he dropped by.

"Hey Ryleigh," Brantley drawled pulling my attention towards him. He smirked up at me as I walked closer. Uh oh, I thought as a long finger pointed at me. "Miss Suzie is highly ticklish. Let's get her."

"Yes!" Ryleigh squealed with glee making Brantley's hat fall off her head as she jumped up. I took off running with a yelp hearing the thunder of feet along with the scrabbling of claws chasing after me. I was in for it now. That was how the rest of the night went. Lots of laughs. I would be scrubbing my kitchen for days to get all the flour from the war Brantley and Ryleigh'd had. But worth it because of the look of pure joy on her little face.

Later that evening, I slowly reached for my phone on the coffee table to snap a picture for Sadie of the view I was seeing from the other end of the couch. Ryleigh was curled in a ball in Brantley's lap sleeping soundly. I'd offered to go lay her down when she first started drifting but he had quickly waved me away. There was no moving for me now at least until we went to bed since my own personal guard dog was holding me down. Spoiled ass even had his own bed in the back of the bakery.

The next night consisted of us getting a first hand dose of handling a sick child. I knew Sadie would freak out but I quickly explained Ryleigh had eaten too many cupcakes when I wasn't looking. The worry and sheepish look on my boyfriend's face proved he had said yes even after I said no. Later that night with the newest princess movie playing on the tv, I met Brantley's eyes over the top of Ryleigh's sleeping form with a smile.

"What?" he asked with a quiet chuckle shifting her head on his shoulder reaching over to toy with the ends of my hair.

"I can see right now," I muttered softly giving him a wink. "If we ever have kids I'm gonna have to be the mean on."

"Says who?" Brantley asked rolling his eyes as I laughed. "Okay. Okay, you probably are right. I would be the total pushover." I nodded leaning down to kiss him softly. When I pulled back he bit his lip looking at me. "That something you want eventually?"

"I do," I answered softly making his smile widen. "In time yea I can see that happening."

November 2014

Brantley's POV

I grabbed the bottle of water Susanna had asked me to get weaving my way through the crowd at the Big Machine afterparty. I could see the fatigue in her eyes knowing she had been busy up until flying out late last night to meet me in Nashville for the CMA's. She and Stephanie were working with the extra staff they had hired for the upcoming holiday season. I was glad that she was delegating more just so she could get a break. Knew she did it to free up time to travel with me. I'd rearranged things to be home or come home more if she was busy.

We'd found our balance on making things work since getting back together. Something that I wished Luke would see that he needed to do more when it came to Sadie. Finding her talking to Kate and Justin, she flashed me a grateful smile as I handed it to her. She'd been less nervous walking tonight's red carpet than she had been for the CMT Awards in June. I still laughed at Sadie telling me about her reaction burying her face in her hands during my performance worried I wouldn't nail the back flip I had done.

"Here baby," I murmured in her ear passing the bottle while wrapping my arms around her. "You okay?"

"Yea B," Susanna answered nodding. "I promise I'm okay. I may sleep the entire way home tomorrow, but I am okay."

"Well I would say if you weren't going home to be elbow deep in pumpkin pies," I teased her earning me an elbow to the ribs. "we could skip town for about a week. Go somewhere warm."

"Hmmm," she sighed as I leaned down kissing her feeling her body relax against mine. "Can I get a raincheck for after Christmas because it does sound like heaven."

"Deal," I promised her as a voice sounded behind us.

"Ahhhh," Scott, my label president, said as he got closer. He leaned down giving Susanna a kiss on the cheek. "There is the lovely baker I was looking for. I stole some of the cupcakes off BG's bus a while. You have an inane talent darlin. My wife was raving about them for weeks. Where did you study?"

"Ummm," Susanna said with a laugh. "My mama and my granny's kitchens. Had plans to study in France for a while but when my business took off there just was never time for it."

"My wife wondered if you ever had," he said with a wink. "Just some of the flavors you used. Listen, I know from what BG has said this is a hectic time of year for you but think I could get you to squeeze in a cake for my wife's birthday?"

"I think I could whip something up," she said with a grin. "Tell me what you had in mind."

Late February 2015

"Dammit Brantley Keith!" Susanna yelled as I hauled ass down my stairs knowing I was in for an ear tug if she got her hands on me right now. "Carl told your dumbass to not sleep on your back last night!! I just bought those sheets too!"

Skidding into the kitchen on my bare feet, I debated pulling out my phone ordering flowers or cookware at this point to get out of trouble with my girlfriend. A snort had me jerking my head up seeing Kolby sitting at the table munching on muffins that Susanna had baked last night. I glared at him only succeeding in making him laugh harder in between bites. I threw my hand up flipping him off wincing a little at the pull on the tender skin of my back. I'd be lucky if Susanna didn't nail me with a wooden spoon in the middle of my newest tattoo just for meanness.

"Shut up," I snarled sitting down beside him slapping his hand away from the last chocolate chip one. "I can't help what I do in my sleep."

"When are you just going to finally ask her to move in?" Kolby asked raising an eyebrow at me. "I mean Susanna spends more time out here now anyways. Why not just bite the bullet?"

"I plan on it," I said dropping my voice glancing towards the doorway making sure Susanna was out of earshot still. "Our anniversary is coming up in May. I plan on asking her a very important question then."

"No shit," he said with wide eyes as I grinned at him. I truthfully didn't want to wait that long but just seemed like the perfect time. "Good. She is the best thing that has ever happened to you bro."

"You just love the fact you get free cupcakes," I snickered feeling his hand squeeze my shoulder. "Wanna go ring shopping with me before I leave for tour rehearsals next week?"

"Damn right," Kolby laughed as we both gulped at the stomping footsteps coming down the stairs. To be so little she could get her point across. "As long as you survive the wrath of Suzie Q. Better find something to appease her."

Know this is just a filler chapter in some ways but trying to move them on along bahaa. Hmmmmm a ring was mentioned......

Put A.....Paris??: Part One

May 2015

Susanna's POV

I felt my heart race making the certified letter in my hands shake. Lifting my eyes, I met Stephanie's who was impatiently waiting to see what I was pale as a ghost for. My mouth opened and closed a few times as I struggled to make my brain form the words. Shock was all that was going through my mind. I wasn't sure I believed things myself. I reached out pinching her arm earning me a smack in return that proved I wasn't dreaming.

"You are going to lose those talented fingers Suz," Stephanie growled trying to grab the letter out of my hands, but I batted her away stepping around the prep table. "What in the world does that letter say?"

"It's a personal offer from Jacques Mormont," I gasped out feeling like my heart was pounding out of my chest. Steph's eyes widened in recognition at the name. Knew I drooled over any new recipe the man shared. Had drug her to Atlanta a few years ago for a seminar he had hosted. Even saying the words out loud didn't sound real. "With a chance to study under him."

"You've said he makes some of the best pastries in the world!" she said. I could see the excitement growing in her eyes. "Susanna! That is amazing!"

"I can't believe it Steph," I murmured reading over the details that it included an option for housing so that ruled out one worry. I swallowed deeply looking up to meet my cousin's eyes shaking my head. "But I can't go."

"Do fucking what!" Stephanie yelled so loud making Katie, our newest high school helper gasp as she grabbed another tray of cupcakes off the counter darting back through the doors. "Like hell you can't! Suz, studying cooking in Paris has always been a dream of yours! I don't want to hear the words you are too old come out of your mouth either! Twenty-seven isn't ancient!" Tears welled in my eyes as I slumped against the counter dropping my head. I sniffled as Stephanie wrapped an arm around me. "What is holding you back?"

"We are expanding," I sighed feeling a yank on my ponytail. "Again. You and Josh can't run three locations without me."

"Like hell we can't," Stephanie argued rolling her eyes. "We've already been doing it. You and I have put a competent team in place Susanna. It's time for you to do something for yourself too. Think of what you can add by studying there. There is already a demand for your specialty wedding cakes all over north Georgia. Soooo what is your next excuse?"

"B," I murmur quietly. Stephanie let out a snort shaking her head. I swear she was two seconds away from chasing me around the kitchen with a rolling pin or a wooden spoon. I was headed to the airport soon to fly out to spend the weekend on the road with him. A cake needing to be finished was the only reason I hadn't left with him yesterday. "We already have one of us gone all the time in this relationship. Don't need both of us."

"You are just asking for that man to turn your ass red aren't you?" she scoffed turning her attention back to icing cookies. "Try and use him for your excuse on not going. I dare you Susanna Grace. He will load you on the plane himself. We both know it. He supports you in anything you set your mind to. You know that. Hell, he and Ben are the ones who scouted the new location closest to campus for us."

"I know he does," I sighed pinching the bridge of my nose in frustration. But this was more than me being busy with orders and him being on the road. This was a year. A freaking year in Paris. "I've got a lot to think about and Jacques, according to this letter, he needs a decision by tomorrow."

"There is no answer but yes Suzie Q," Stephanie sighed shaking her head then pointed to the door. "Go on and get out of here. Straight to the airport. Enjoy your weekend okay."

"Okay, okay," I laughed untying my apron before heading into my office to grab my things. I knew I had a lot to think about on my flight to Dallas regardless of what Stephanie said. I mean could I really just up and leave my family, my boyfriend, and my business for a year? Yea, there was a lot of potential to come from me studying there but still. I'd already seen Brantley's tentative schedule for this fall going into next year. It was packed. All of that plus him spending so much time in Alabama getting the farm he bought running like he wanted. I was so damn proud of what he had planned for that. My hands shook slightly as I drove. What was he going to say about all this if I left for a year?

Brantley's POV

"You want to stop pacing Boss," PJ snickered walking on my bus making me whirl around glaring at him. "It's time for soundcheck."

"I know," I muttered slipping my sunglasses on following him out to the golf cart parked by my bus. We rode in silence for a minute before PJ decided to voice his opinion on my nerves.

"You got a plan in place BG," he laughed as I growled rubbing my hand over my jean pocket feeling the shape of the ring box resting there. I'd been hiding it at the house praying Susanna didn't exactly discover it. "You know Cupcake will say yes so stop freaking out man."

"Yea well," I grumbled bouncing my leg nervously. "She may say no."

"Yea....okay," PJ said with a snort climbing off the golf cart trailing after me to the stage. I tried to calm my racing heart reminding myself that I had nothing to worry about. No doubt in my mind that she loved me. A smile twitched at my lips as I walked off stage after finishing soundcheck. Leaned against one of the equipment cases was Susanna grinning as Brittany showed her something on her phone. No doubt wedding photos since she and Jason were still in that newlywed bubble. Made the itch to pull the ring box out of my pocket even worse. I wanted that with her so badly. But there was timing to everything I knew. Like she sensed me coming, her head lifted up as I got closer.

A beautiful smile that I wanted to see everyday for the rest of my life. Brittany gave me a wink turning to go find Jason as I wrapped my arms around Susanna claiming her lips with mine. I'd only left yesterday but damn did I miss this no matter how long I was gone. Losing myself I deepened the kiss stepping forward to press her back against the case eliminating all space between us. Slim hands pushed against my chest with a laugh as Susanna blinked up at me fanning her face. I smirked at her sliding my fingers along the waistband of her jeans hooking them in her belt loops.

"Barely been twenty-four hours B," she said shaking her head. "Missed me that bad?"

"Desperately," I teased her kissing her again. Stepping back, I laced my fingers with hers pulling her down the corridor to find the door leading to the buses. She silently fell in step with me. Something was off with her, but I wasn't sure what. She pulled away from me as we walked on the bus puffing out a breath. A frown marred my face as she put her back to me wringing her hands together. "Susanna, what is wrong baby girl?" She spun around with wide eyes biting her bottom lip. "Don't try and tell me something isn't bothering you either."

"B," she murmured walking over to her bag on the couch opening it. "We need to talk."

"Nothing good ever comes from those words," I grumbled crossing my arms seeing her face pale at my words instantly making me feel like hell. I shook off the feeling of impending doom schooling the worry on my face. "Go ahead baby. What do you need to say?"

"Here," Susanna said handing me the letter she had pulled out of her bag. I took it from her trembling hand trying to keep it together for her. As I read my eyes grew wide. I pointed at the name on the letter head.

"Isn't this the French dude that has the cake pan line you swear by baby?" I asked her looking up seeing amber eyes roll at me before she nodded. "The one I remember shelling out a pretty penny on for your birthday last month. Need to tell him it's just a cake pan baby, not gold bricks." Susanna reached out smacking the back of my head as I cracked up laughing. "So Paris huh?"

"I think I'm going to pass on it," Susanna whispered so softly I almost didn't hear her. Like hell she was. I stepped forward pulling her into my arms settling down on the couch with her in my arms. Nervous fingers toyed with my necklace as I tipped her face up to look at me. "It's a year B. In France. I mean..."

"It's a dream of yours baby," I said forcing a reassuring smile on my face. "You can't pass that up. If I'm the reason you haven't jumped on this then baby, don't let me hold you back. Go for It."

"It means me being there," she argued gripping the end of my chin staring at me hard. "You being here. I've seen your schedule...."

"And I will shift some things if I have to," I reminded her. We would figure something out. "I'll be in Europe at the end of the year anyhow. By then you should know all the places to visit. Be my own personal tour guide." I wiggled my eyebrows at her making a giggle slip out. "Maybe developed a sexy French accent."

"You're ridiculous," Susanna laughed shaking her head. But the worry in her eyes eased so mission accomplished. "You are really okay with me doing this?"

"Baby," I said cupping her face kissing her slowly. "I love you. You are my forever. That means I also am not standing in the way of your dreams. We've got this."

"Love you too," she sighed burying her face in my neck hugging me tight. "I'm gonna miss you."

Later that night, I looked down at Susanna's sleeping face feeling the reality of our situation. Smoothing a hand over her soft skin, she snuggled closer making my heart twist. Well, that ring burning a hole in my pocket earlier would have to wait a while longer. No way I could ask her. At least not right now. Susanna would pass on the opportunity if I did. I meant what I said on supporting her. If the shoe was on the other foot she would do the same for me with no hesitation. Looked like I would be racking up the frequent flyer miles for the next year when my schedule would let me. But damn, she was worth it.

I shall be joining in the teepee......hope there is some wine left

Put A....Paris??: Part Two

December 2015

Brantley's POV

I tried to keep my excitement in as we landed in Amsterdam knowing I was getting just a little bit closer to seeing my girl. Turning my phone on as we walked through the terminal, I smiled at the photo on my lock screen that Susanna had sent me a while back. White chef jacket on, auburn hair in a messy bun, and as always flour on her cheek. But the look of pure joy doing something that she loved made it worth the missing her. I'd been busy enough that the last six months had flown by. But tonight, damn I'd finally get to lay eyes on her and it not be through a phone or computer screen. Ben let out a laugh at the cheesy grin on my face rolling his eyes.

"Well, well," he laughed throwing an arm around my shoulders. "Dare I say this is the biggest grin I have seen on your face since before Suzie Q got on that plane in May? Kind of missed her too. Think my girlfriend works even more now then she did before she left though."

"I think Steph tells you that so she can get a break from your aggravating ass," I snickered making Ben tap his chin thoughtfully before shrugging. "I know her wanting to stay close for Sadie is the only reason she didn't tag along on this trip." My phone chimed with an incoming text making me roll my eyes. "And speaking of Sadie."

"Got all the good European chocolate places researched huh," Ben laughed reading over my shoulder. "Yep we better not forget that or I foresee bodily harm in our future."

"Good that you know this is on both of us then," I chuckled grabbing my luggage falling in line with the rest of the guys trailing behind Rich. After getting checked in our hotel, we headed to the venue next door to run through a quick soundcheck. My phone buzzing in my pocket had me yanking it out grinning see Susanna's name. I tugged my in ears out heading offstage to answer it. PJ gave me a broad grin as I passed him. I was radiating with excitement as I answered. "Hey baby! Your train made it yet? Rich was making sure that....."

"B," Susanna sighed quietly in my ear. I froze in my tracks as my gut twisted knowing I wasn't going to like what she said next. "I tried calling earlier but you were still in the air I guess. Look...I have this group project that has come up. We have to make a souffle presentation at Jacques's restaurant tomorrow night. The recipe he has given us to work on is the most complicated I have ever seen. I'm not going to be able to make it tonight baby."

"What?" I growled unable to keep myself from snapping at her. "We've only had all this setup for two months Susanna! I haven't seen you in six months. Fuck woman do you realize how much I miss you!"

"And you think I don't!" she yelled back. "You've at least been in familiar territory. Close to home! I've had a whole fucking ocean between me and everyone I know and love! Baking and learning has been the only thing that has kept me going B. I'm so damn homesick it has been miserable."

"Well you are the one who chose to go!" I snapped back turning to bang my fist on the wall closest to me. A growl vibrated in my ear reminding me the woman on the other end of the line didn't take my shit on a good day. I swallowed deeply trying to reign in my temper and disappointment. I had kept busy since I watched her walk through the gates boarding the plane headed to France. Did that and kept reminding myself we had this. She dealt with me being going for my career all the time. I could do the same for her. "Suzie Q...."

"Save it," she hissed with so much venom my jaw dropped. "You supported me on this remember Brantley Keith. Think of all the times you've had to rearrange plans we had because of an interview coming up. You think I'm not disappointed!"

"Baby," I sighed pinching the bridge of my nose in frustration. I just wanted her in my arms. Even if was just for a night. It would get me through the next few months. "I know..." I was cut off by a booming laugh in the background followed by the familiar clank of dishes. Heard a deep voice calling for Susanna to hurry up. The words out of my mouth next firmly lodged my boot in there but I saw red not caring. "Well, seems you are busy darlin. Don't let me keep you. Good luck on your presentation. Call me when you have time for your boyfriend."

"B!" she gasped but I didn't let her finished before I ended the call turning to punch the wall this time before stomping back to the stage. Ben was idly twirling his drumsticks waiting on me to get back. Jesse's eyes narrowed as I got closer.

"Please tell me Suzie Q has made it and bringing goodies?" Ben asked. I swear I could see the drool slipping down his chin. Stephanie used the same recipes so I knew he wasn't starving by any means. I growled at him making his eyes widen. "Fine! Okay! I'll share man don't bite my hand off."

"She's not coming," I snapped grabbing my guitar and circling my hand in the air. "Let's get this run through so I can go grab a cigarette before doing interviews."

Susanna's POV

Shifting my bag on my shoulder, I pushed the curled strands of hair away from my face as I followed Rich through the back door of the venue in Hamburg. Guilt had eaten at me the last few days. My phone calls and texts going unanswered. I knew Brantley was pissed and disappointed. Also was betting he felt a little like he wasn't a priority. One extreme ass chewing from a very grumpy Sadie had sent me dialing Rich's number to make sure I was able to come to this show. I didn't have to fly back to Paris until late tomorrow night.

The closer we got to the room Rich said they were hanging out in before the show, the more my hands shook. Six months. Six long months since I had seen my boyfriend face to face. I honestly was worried though. I could feel us slipping. Something we both had promised wouldn't happen to us. Not after fighting so hard to make things work. Marco and Katherine my project partners had been giving me hell for months about the fact my boyfriend hadn't even come to visit me.

How does one explain to two European strangers that he can't come visit because he is on tour? Finally I had just explained to Katherine to just Google him. Her jaw had dropped then asked me if was making shit up. That was until she got a good look at the picture of Brantley and Sylo on my phone. I stopped in the hallway staring at the door feeling my stomach roll with what I was hoping was butterflies.

"He's gonna be excited to see you," Rich said giving me a reassuring smile. I bit my lip taking a deep breath as he opened the door.

"Not so sure about that," I mumbled following him in. My frantic eyes swept the room for Brantley but came up empty making my heart drop.

"Suzie Q!" Ben yelled jumping to his feet running across the room sweeping me up in a bear hug. I felt him spin me around and I couldn't help but laugh. I ruffled his mohawk that I didn't even get growled at for. Guess he had missed me. Sitting me down on my feet I got a wink. "I missed you so much I will let that slide."

"There's Cupcake," PJ chuckled hugging me tight kissing the top of my head. "Boss will be glad to see you."

"I hope," I whispered under my breath hearing boots scrape as the door opened again. Brantley walked in rolling his eyes at something on his phone. He paused as he looked up seeing me stand there. The range of emotions going through his eyes made my heart race. My eyes welled with tears of relief of being this close to him. My stomach soured as he locked down his feelings and narrowed his eyes.

"Susanna," he said gruffly. I swallowed deeply. Shit. He was pissed. No hey baby, I've missed you or anything. "Surprised you could find the time."

"B," I whimpered shaking my head to clear the brewing tears. "I..."

"Not fair Boss," PJ snapped thumping the back of Brantley's head as he motioned for the guys to follow him out. "You make Cupcake cry and we will have words. Come on y'all lets give them the room." We both stood motionless as the band trailed after PJ. Ben shot me a sad smile before shutting the door. I shuffled my feet back and forth as Brantley shoved his hands in his pockets not meeting my eyes. It was deathly quiet for what felt like forever.

This wasn't quite the reception I had expected. Feeling myself grow angry at the hurt I was feeling because I expected better from him. This wasn't us. We weren't petty like this. We talked about things even after we finished yelling at each other. Regardless of his reasons, him closing me off was unacceptable. Throwing my shoulders back I mustered up all the wounded pride I could.

"I'll just go," I said quietly doing everything in my power to keep my voice neutral. I kept my eyes on the floor so I wouldn't break as I scurried towards the door. Maybe I could catch a redeye out to Paris hopefully. I'd be able to get back and bake my feelings away. "Guess I shouldn't have come."I yanked the door open only to have a hand reach above me slamming it shut. Resting my forehead on the smooth wood, I was unable to stop the sniffle that slipped out. Feeling myself turned, a calloused finger tipped my chin up.

Lips claimed mine giving me what I had been craving for months. Brantley kissed me like a dying man in a desert finding that final drink of water. My bag slid to the floor as I pushed up wrapping my arms around his neck trying to get closer. Buried in the arms I had missed desperately I felt better than I had since before boarding that plane out of Atlanta. Tears slipped down my cheeks as my chest heaved.

I missed the texts I used to wake up to everyday that because of the time difference for us had tapered off. Missed the random stupid shit he and Kolby came up to do when he was home. A sob slipped past my lips making Brantley lift his head looking down at me. He reached up wiping the tears that were streaming down my cheeks away with a sigh.

"Don't cry baby," he murmured pressing his forehead to mine wrapping me up a little tighter. "I was being an ass. Fuck. I am so sorry."

"I let you down," I argued clinging to him. "I'm the one who is sorry. I tried. I hope you know that."

"I know baby girl," Brantley said giving me a soft smile. "I just have missed you so fucking much. Mama swears she doesn't know who pouts worse. Me or Sylo. That damn dog has been lost without you baby."

"I've missed him too," I sighed with a quiet laugh snuggling closer to him as he stood there holding me. "Your mama was telling me it was pretty sad when I talked to her the other day. How is Sadie?"

"As well as can be expected," he reassured me. I knew between him, the boys, Tiffany, and Stephanie she was well taken care of. "Royal pain in my ass some days."

"Just a little bit longer," I snickered knowing the hell she had been raising. A quiet knock sounded on the other side of the door that I was all too familiar with. Brantley glared at the unseen person on the other side before leaning down to kiss me again making my toes curl in my boots. I pulled away grazing my teeth over his bottom lip earning me a playful growl that I had missed. "That's your cue outlaw. Come on before PJ sends out a search party."

"Yes mam," Brantley grinned twining his fingers with mine as I opened the door. A hard smack across my jean clad ass made me jump with a shriek. "See that bossiness is still there. But God knows, I wouldn't trade it for anything in the world." He leaned down kissing my cheek as we walked. "I love you Susanna."

"Love you too B," I sighed happily praying this giddy feeling I hadn't felt in months lasted. "Don't you forget it."

At least she finally made it. Hmmm...Sadie laid down the law didn't she. Keep up to date with her by checking out Crash My Party from . There could be evilness afoot

Almost Within Reach

A delirious laugh slipped past my lips followed by a deep chuckle that made a smile twist along my lips. Lord how I had missed that sound. After a rough start, things had been getting better. The heat from his stare anytime he'd glance to the wings during his show tonight had me squirming and on edge. One thing was for certain, I had missed him body and soul. Sliding my hands down, I slipped them into the back pockets of Brantley's jeans knowing I was thoroughly distracting him as he fumbled to open the door to his hotel room. The strap of my bag slipping off his shoulder.

"Woman," he grunted using his shoulder to push the door open making me slip digging my fingers into his shirt to keep from falling. "You are playing with fire."

"Don't tell me that you are complaining," I teased with a giggle. Spinning around he kicked the door closed with a slamming thud in his hurry. Muttering silky threats that made me hum and whimper at the same time. My feet had barely touched the carpet before B's lips were on mine. Tongues tangling. Teeth gnashing. One of those deeply possessive kisses that rocked you to your core. Like you both were doing your level best to crawl inside each other. Fingers buried in my hair yanking my head back giving him better access.

"Fuck, I have missed you," Brantley murmured breaking the kiss raising his head to look down. I couldn't keep in the moan as his eyes trailed over me. Biting my bottom lip, I gripped then ends of his t-shirt yanking it over his head taking his hat with it. Eyes closed tightly, groaning as I leaned forward kissing my way across his chest undoing his belt before flicking the button on his jeans. Feeling empowered in the fact that once, I had him hanging on by a thread, I eased my hand into the parted denim circling the velvety steel shaft feeling his body tremble. "Dammit Susanna..."

"Hmmm..."I teased coyly looking up at him. Noticing the chair out of the corner of my eye, I raised an eyebrow pointing to it. "Go have a seat baby."

"Huh?" Brantley gasped then growled when I ceased my torturous movements on his dick. I ducked out of his arms with a laugh shoving him forward. Giggling the whole time as he grumbled and stumbled kicking his socks and boots off. He dropped down in the comfy wing back chair leaning back crooking his finger at me. "Come here."

"You aren't running this show," I smirked seeing aroused green eyes narrowing at me. He shrugged sliding his hand into his jeans leaning back making me growl. "Hands off what is mine."

"Then you better stop ya teasing baby girl and come claim it then," he said in a seductive whisper that sent a trembling shiver through my body. Keeping my eyes locked with his, I tugged my shirt over my head then quickly shed my jeans and boots. Saw Brantley's chest heave in anticipation as I stood there in the sheer black lace matching set. Eyes trailing over me making my aching nipples throb just from the heat in his eyes. That right there was the look I had been needing. The one that I had been missing all of our months apart. The look still stating he wanted me more than anything. Biting his lip he shook his head. "If you want any chance of those staying in one piece then lose them as you walk Susanna. Or I'm going to shred them into pieces."

Nodding my head in understanding, I reached back flipping the hooks on the bra taking my time to let it slip down my arms hitting the floor. I stepped closer so turned on the nerves I'd had earlier today about being with him again disappearing. Watched him push his hands down sending his jeans to the floor before resuming his appeared relaxed position. Hard dick standing at full attention begging for me. We both knew we were anything but relaxed.

Stopping in front of Brantley, I turned shaking my hair back over my shoulder trailing my fingers down my sides hooking into the thin straps at my hips before bending over all the way giving my extremely turned on boyfriend a full glistening view of just how much my damp pussy had missed him. Arms wrapped around me with a growl yanking me down into his lap. As he lifted, I pushed my legs up letting out a quiet scream as he impaled me in one deep thrust growling in my ear. That sound always assured to do nothing but make me wetter every time. Judging by the devilish chuckle, he knew it too.

Lifting my arms back, I wrapped them around his neck connecting us as his lips ghosted along my skin heightening the pleasure. Using his big body as leverage, I began to move. Long fingers dug into my hips hanging on for dear life as much as guiding me. One big hand lifted tangling into my loose hair tugging my head to the side as lips claimed mine. A kiss so raw, so undeniably passionate that if I had been standing, I would have collapsed to the floor. I pushed down riding him as he pushed up meeting me with each determined thrust.

Right now wasn't about taking our time. Showing the other how much we loved each other. We both knew that. This, this was about raw want and need. Satisfying a craving for the connection we shared after being apart from months. The sound of skin slamming against skin. Chasing the heights of pleasure, we only ever found with each other.

Brantley gripped my hips slamming me down hard on him as I came so hard out of nowhere stars exploded behind my eyes. Teeth sank into my shoulder blade as he followed me over the precipice of untamed desire with a growl. I collapsed back against him my body trembling. Chest heaving, I melted back against his warm, sweat slicked chest with a sigh.

"Damn I needed that," I moaned lacing my fingers with his on my stomach. I felt a smile on his lips that were pressed against my skin. Squeezing his hands, I held tight wanting these moments and memories to get me through the next few months. My eyes burned with tears knowing I was getting what felt like so little time before we were separated again. "I love you."

"Not as much as I love you," Brantley chuckled kissing my neck before shifting me in his arms to stand. I knew with no doubt in my mind that big bed beside us was his intended destination.

Brantley's POV

Laying on our sides, I idly swirled my finger along the cursive script on Susanna's ribs. I vaguely remembered my surprise discovering her tattoo there. I can do all things through Him who strengthens me. Philippians 4:13. But it suited her perfectly. A content sigh puffed from her kiss swollen lips making me chuckle as I leaned forward brushing a soft kiss along her shoulder.

"I don't want to go back," Susanna whispered snuggling closer into me. I didn't want her to go back either, but things were what they were for now. "I've missed you so much."

"I know baby," I sighed rolling to my back settling her across my chest as I ghosted my fingers along her skin. "But just a couple weeks and you will be home for Christmas. I know a certain dog that will be beyond excited to see you."

"About that," Susanna whispered so lowly I almost didn't hear it. Tumbled auburn hair shook back as she raised her head looking at me. "I'm not getting to come home for Christmas."

"Huh?" I asked in disbelief. She had to be kidding me. We had been looking forward to her being in for the holidays. Made plans with both our families. Had every intention on lighting a fire in the early hours of Christmas morning, making love to her right there by the fireplace then asking her to be mine forever. Susanna sat up biting her lip. Amber eyes welling with tears. "We had this planned Susanna. It even said in the letter you were getting a holiday break!"

"I know but," she sighed looking down at her hands. "I got offered the chance to sous chef for Jacques in his restaurant on Christmas Eve. That means being able to plan the dessert menu Brantley! Do you not understand what a big deal this is for me! The notoriety it could bring if all goes well."

"All I am hearing is that you could have said no," I growled through clenched teeth glaring up at her. "Fuck Susanna! Do you not realize how much you are missed at home? Any care of how excited Ryleigh was about you coming home! All I heard about once I told her was getting Miss Suzie home to help her make Christmas cookies!"

"And I can do them next year!" Susanna snapped crossing her arms over her heaving bare chest. "This is a big thing for me Brantley! Maybe I could have said no, but I didn't. How many times have you been in the same situation! I remember you missing my birthday this year because of interviews! But I understood because it was part of your career. Sometimes I wonder if we even want the same things anymore!"

"I know that I want you," I argued back closing my eyes in frustration. Felt my temper rage but knew I didn't want to spend what little time I had with her fighting. The quiet sniffle echoing through the quiet hotel room made me sigh. I opened my eyes lifting my arms. I banded them around Susanna pulling her into my side as she burrowed closer. Kissing the top of her silky hair, I did my best to make peace for now. What worried me was I felt her slipping away from me. We had either been fighting or missing each other's calls lately. "Let's table this for tonight baby. I don't want to be fighting with you during what little time we have."

"Me either," she sniffled clinging to me. "I don't want to either but..."

"Not tonight Susanna," I grumbled harsher than I meant too. "We will talk later."

The next morning, I lifted my head off the pillow blinking against the bright sunlight. Raising my head up, I glanced around for Susanna then listened to see if I heard the shower running. Didn't surprise me that she would wake up before me. Laying face down, I stretched my arms out wincing a little against the scratch marks she had put there early this morning. My fingers brushed smooth paper making me sit up as I yanked it to me.

Eyes burned with tears as I saw my name before unfolding it. Reading wounded me to the core and cracked my heart wide open. I can't believe her! Jumping out of bed, I paced the room lashing out at anything I could find. Sending odds and ends hurtling across the room. My boot crashed into the television with a booming crack that I didn't even care. Left me. Ended things! Said that we seemed to not want the same things anymore. Why couldn't I support her!

With a roar I stalked to the shower with the intent of washing last night off me. Fucking chicken shit is what she was! Thought she loved me! Later I was stuffing the last of my things into my bag when a knock sounded on the door. I yanked it open with a snarl then felt my face fall in disappointment seeing PJ there. He let out a low whistle as he stepped into the room.

"Damn Boss," he said with a booming laugh giving me a wink about the trashed room. "You and Cupcake get a little wild last night. She ready to head to the airport."

"She's gone," I snapped making his jaw drop. "Fucking let me with nothing but a goddamn note. Gone before I woke back up earlier."

"Maybe..."PJ started to say but I cut him off with a glare grabbing my things heading to the door. "Well okay then. Let's go."

Covers ears and runs to the teepee.... save me!!!!

The Outlaw and The Ass Shaker: Round 1

Brantley's POV

Hearing the crinkle of the wrapper for the expensive ass chocolate Ben had reminded me to buy, I rolled my eyes at the low moan. Of course, Sadie had been the resident chocaholic of Jackson County since finding out she was pregnant. I had forgotten to drop the box off the other day after I dropped in to check on her and Ryleigh once I got home. Sometimes I wished she didn't know that I had a key to the bakery. All three of them. I frowned looking down at my hands. Not like I would need them anymore. Sylo walked closer laying his black and white head on my knee puffing out a sigh. Ryleigh had begged for him to stay with them while I was gone. Sad eyes looked up at me. Like umm...where is she?

My jaw clenched thinking of waking up finding Susanna gone. One scathing voicemail is all that I had left before getting on the plane bound home. The words in that letter haunted me every waking moment. Not like I had slept much since getting back anyways. PJ had been concerned I'd wind up on the no-fly list because someone even breathing wrong had pissed me off. I'd been avoiding Mama saying I was tired the last couple of days to keep her from finding out. Connie had text me this morning asking if Susanna had sent a gift she needed home with me. I had just answered no mam she didn't.

Susanna could deal with the repercussions from her mama on her own. I hated it for them when she called to give the news she wasn't coming home. Bad enough that I would be the one to break it to Ryleigh. Why didn't she get it through her stubborn head that people were looking forward to seeing her? Had missed her. Hell, I had been more involved in Sadie's pregnancy than her own best friend!

"Mmmm..." Sadie sighed making me look up meeting her inquisitive blue eyes. "Don't tell Luke but my God these are even better than the ones he dropped off from New York last week." Sitting the box down she rested her hands on the swell of her stomach giving me her undivided attention. Shit. "Alright, you have been grumpier than normal since getting back. How is our world traveling baker doing? Know she will be glad to set foot in Georgia next week. Almost as glad as you will be to have her home for the holidays."

"How did the ultrasound appointment go?" I asked changing the subject not wanting to talk about it. Blue eyes narrowed at me before looking around. "What Sadie?"

"Umm well..." she murmured tapping a finger on the table. "About that... ..."I narrowed my eyes. I know she didn't lie to me. "Luke didn't come okay. There was a tour date changed he forgot about." I let out a low snarl making her glower prompting me I was probably two seconds away from an ear tug. "How about you stop changing the subject! You've been a grouchy ass. I know you had to have gotten laid. So I will ask about Susanna again...."

"She's not coming," I growled lowly feeling my fists clench. I just needed to hit something. Anything to lessen the ache in my chest. If I just thought things ending last time was bad, this was way worse. Sure, there had been a time or two one of us had walked out after a fight. Okay, maybe there had been a day or two in between those times that it seemed like the whole town waited with bated breath to see who would cave first on apologizing. But it was different this time. Hell I'd had the proposal all worked out in my mind down to the very last detail. I heard Sadie gasp making my head lift meeting her eyes. "She's not coming home. Some important opportunity with that French jackass came up."

"Damn B," Sadie sighed shaking her head. "I'm sorry. Know you were excited to have her home. But you got a couple days with her right. She was flying to meet you in Hamburg after that project came up."

"A night," I mumbled my voice cracking slightly as memories clouded my mind. Having her close enough to touch after so long had seemed unreal. "I got barely a night before she left."

"Well she is..." she started to say but I cut her off with a shake of my head.

"I mean she left Sadie," I explained drumming my fingers on the kitchen table. "I rolled over to reach for her finding cold sheets and a fucking Dear John note!" My fist slammed down making Sadie jerk with a gasp. I'd tried everything just short of burying myself in a bottle which had bigger repercussions for everyone if I were to do that. Puffing out a heaving sigh, I leaned forward bracing my hands on my knees closing my eyes. A second later soft hands settled over mine making my eyes open. The tenderness and worry in Sadie's baby blues that were brimming with tears hurt. I should be worried about upsetting her in her condition. Not drowning in my own heartache.

"Oh BG," she muttered softly squeezing before lifting one hand up to cup my cheek. That one right there had all the tough guy walls I prided myself on cracking. Other than PJ, she was the first one I had admitted Susanna had broken up with me to. Truthfully that term wasn't good enough.

Broke my heart. Shattered it into a million pieces was more like it. Sadie let out a quiet mutter. "I swear when she comes home I'm gonna..."

"Don't," I murmured lifting my hand up to circle her wrist forcing a sad smile. "I appreciate it darlin but don't ruin your friendship over me okay."

"Yea well you're my friend too," Sadie argued raising an eyebrow at me. "You've been so great to me. To Ryleigh. Susanna, well....."

"Well what do we have here?" Luke snapped from the kitchen doorway dropping his bag down with a thud crossing his arms glaring at Sadie and I both. She gasped letting her hands fall taking a step away. He had to be kidding me right now. Nope, those brown eyes were narrowed to slits aimed straight at me. His chest puffed out a little trying to be intimidating. Key word here...trying. "What would your girlfriend say BG? Susanna is thousands of miles away and look at you getting....."

"That's it!" I roared diving around Sadie raising my fist as I moved. She let out a scream as I decked Luke sending him crashing onto the tile floor. Bracing one hand in the middle of his chest, I reared back to nail him again hearing her cry out and my friend's eyes widen in disbelief.

"Don't break his face BG!" Sadie yelled making my head whip around. Which gave Luke the opportunity to clock my jaw knocking me off of him. Well, well the ass shaker had a decent right hook. We rolled around trading licks. I felt a rib crack as Luke got a couple good swings in before I flipped him off me right after he punched my nose making me see stars. I had been spoiling for a fight ever since Susanna left. Came close to beating Ben on the drive home from the airport but Stephanie had threatened to make both of us walk all the way home from Atlanta.

I was drawn back to punch Luke again knowing it would knock him out. His brown eyes widened seeing the glinting silver of my rings. A piercing whistle made both of us jump. "THOMAS LUTHER! BRANT-

LEY KEITH! STOP THIS SHIT RIGHT NOW!" What made both of us whip our heads around was the groan of pain immediately following the yell. Sadie wrapped one arm around her stomach turning pale while gripping a chair for dear life with the other. "Hospital...now!"

"Shit!" Luke and I yelled in unison jumping up from the floor. I scurried towards the door holding is as she waddled after me. Luke resting a comforting hand on her back meeting my eyes in real fear.

Sadie's POV( )

The comforting sound of the fetal heart monitor has me constantly rubbing my large belly knowing that everything is okay with baby boy. When the doctor nonchalantly said it was just round ligament pain, I wanted to throw something at him. However, I wanted to duck and hide when he said I was dehydrated and my blood pressure was elevated. Told me I needed to reduce my stress and watch my salt intake. Luke and Brantley simultaneously growled hearing the doctor mention it. Pfft... decreasing my stress is not that easy. Limiting my salt? Fine. But my stress... yea right.

My stress is a walk in the park right now compared to the bombshell Brantley dropped on me before him and Luke decided to act like children. No wonder why he acted strange after returning from his trip. Honestly thought the man would have been glowing like a teenage boy who just lost his virginity. Highly the opposite. I should have known when he changed the subject on me when he first came by after returning home.

Kind of brushed it off like he didn't just return from seeing Susanna who he has missed like crazy. He was also grumpier than his usual grumpiness. He can be a little grumpy but lately the man has been a crotchety old geezer. Brantley gives me a tight lipped smile noticing me looking him over. The lights in the hospital make his dark circles more prominent adding to the heart ache I'm feeling for him.

"Woman," chuckled Brantley. "Stop giving me that look. Don't be worrying over me. You heard the doc. Start reducing that stress."

"Yea," Luke mumbled. He puffs out a heavy sigh pushing up from the chair. "You need to come out to stay with me, Sadie."

"Don't start on that again," I growled. I snap my neck at the snickering coming from my right. "You find this funny?"

"Go live with your baby daddy for awhile and have his ass make your food runs," Brantley leans back in the chair with a big grin on his face.

"Oh darlin quick question," Luke diverts my attention from trying to reach for Brantley's ear from the hospital bed. "Why did you tell BG here not to mess up my face but didn't say anything to me of doing the same?" Luke arches a brow stepping closer to the bed. Brantley starts cracking up in the chair right as the nurse comes in with my discharge papers.

"Don't make me answer that," I winced trying not to hurt his ego any more than I already did. That added more to Brantley's booming laugh that has the nurse blush and take note of him. The flirty grin she tosses his way has me ready to smack Susanna upside her head when she returns home. "Nah uh, he's taken so step back," I snapped. The nurse gives Brantley one more longing glance before coming to remove my IV and take off the monitoring strapped around my abdomen so I can get the hell out of here. I swear she rips the tape off just perfectly to give me a little sting. She even gives Luke the same grin she gave Brantley as she steps away from the bed that has me almost lunge at her. Brantley clamps his hand down on my knee giving me a look to cool it. When she finally leaves purposely swinging her hips, my hormones have had enough shit for the night. "Damnit one of y'all best be bringing me to get food. Little man and I are hungry."

Walking out of the hospital doesn't go unnoticed by this small town. Several onlookers whispering and people holding up their phones greet us through the walk out the hospital. Oh I can hear it now... who is the father? Is it Luke or BG? Luke's arm around my waist should answer that question but with a certain outlaw at my house more than the daddy well it causes people to talk. Now that Susanna has been gone also doesn't help the gossiping committee. Once word of their break up makes its way through this town it's going to be even more ridiculous.

Kicks from baby boy have me giggling in the middle of eating my fries and milkshake in the passenger seat of Brantley's truck. Luke leans up from the back seat resting his hand on my stomach. When he sits back I glance over at Brantley who gives me a grin then makes it disappear when he looks ahead at the road. Poor guy. He and I have our own lonely hearts club. I've been stubborn I know that. After my trip to Tennessee though, I still cannot help but to feel weary about the man sitting behind me who occasionally twirls my hair that I don't bother stopping. Even after Brantley set me straight over my freakout from the movie theater. Now that him and Susanna are broken up I have a feeling he's going to be more on Team Luke than Team Sadie. That is until Luke does something...again.

Welll...that went down . Think he isn't handling it too well. Thank you for supplying Sadie's POV of how he is dealing with things. Stay tuned to her Crash My Party for the latest with Luke and Sadie

Not A Warm Welcome: Part I

June 2016

Susanna's POV

I winced hearing the front door of the bakery slam as Sadie stalked out. Doing my best to bury down the guilt, I tried to not think about all I had missed from being gone. Before I even made it back into the kitchen Steph started in. I just leaned against the counter letting her have it. I pursed my lips listening to Stephanie complain at me for what felt like the thousandth time since I had made it home two weeks ago.

Do believe she had yelled I was too Frenchiefied while throwing a wooden spoon at my head the other day. Needless to say she'd shipped me off to the location near campus for the next few days stating she had our Jefferson location firmly in hand. Honestly made me feel like my presence wasn't wanted in this whole town. While a bakery had been my dream, it wouldn't be a reality without Stephanie. Or having more than one location now. Steph was the one who kept things running while I had been in France. I owed her and Josh so damn much.

It was a slightly chilly homecoming to say the least. While Mama and Daddy were thrilled I was home, the sting of me missing Christmas was surely felt. Granny Hale had looked like she swallowed a bitter pecan when she opened the bottle of French perfume I had brought her for a late birthday present. Reminded me of her because of the smell along with the elegant crystal bottle. Swore I heard her mutter she would have rather settled for a dozen of my macaroons instead. I'd yet to have seen Brantley which I was dreading.

Sadie had quit answering my calls or texts after I had missed Bo's birth. I wasn't even here for Tiffany's going away party since she accepted that job in Atlanta. We'd gone to dinner the other night but things were off with her as well. I felt a million miles away from everyone and everything that I had missed being across the ocean. Snapping fingers pulled me from my deep thoughts. I lifted my head seeing Stephanie's glare darken.

"And another thing," she snapped motioning at me. "What the hell is that outfit? Since when have you ever worn a skirt to work? A black one at that with..is that kitten heels? What the fuck Suz? This isn't you!"

"What does it hurt to look nicer for our customers?" I snarled back putting my hands on my hips. My cousin scoffed with a shake of her head before going back to work kneading the dough before her. I walked over bracing my hands on the counter meeting her glare head on. "I can't change things up."

"Change things up huh?" Stephanie asked through clenched teeth. "No, what has happened is you have changed! This is not you Susanna! France changed you!"

"Did not!" I argued back. I had heard the same muttered remark from our own grandmother the other day. "There is a life outside this small town Steph. You used to dream of leaving too!"

"Well if you loved it so much you should have stayed," she hissed making me gasp. Stephanie closed her eyes with a sigh shaking her head before opening them again. "I'm sorry Suz. I shouldn't have said that. You followed your dream. No one can fault you for that."

"But what can you fault me for?" I asked in a wounded voice. Her words cut deeper than I wanted to admit to myself. "You pushed me to go. I learned a lot over there. Stuff that really can set us apart."

"Yes you did," she admitted with a nod. "I love some of the new recipes you have created or found. The ones you sent me to incorporate have been a hit. But there also are staple favorites. I'm scared you forgot your roots Susanna. You never dressed like this for work unless for a luncheon. And then you changed so fast my head would spin. I miss the Susanna that loved to bake barefoot. Who thrived on the kids coming in for the latest cupcake creation. This French music is not soothing. It's annoying as shit. There any reason you changed it from the local country station the other day?"

"No," I growled through clenched teeth stalking past Stephanie to kick off the heels in my office. I stomped back out rolling my eyes knowing exactly what she was referring to. This part of Georgia you can damn sure bet that Brantley was all over the radio. "Has nothing to do with him."

"Oh darlin," Stephanie chuckled as I washed my hands before turning to get busy as well shaking my chin length hair out of the way. "This has everything to do with Brantley. Guess it's a good thing he has been on the road since you blew back into town. I'm betting that run in is going to be explosive. What happened? I never really found out. You sounded so down around Christmas then like a different person after that."

"I ended things," I muttered with an absent shrug knowing that was a chicken shit answer. Biting the inside of my cheek I tamped down the hurt flowing through me. Swallowing deeply I continued. "I took the chicken shit route leaving him a note." Stephanie growled at me making me feel even worse. "I know. I know."

"No," Stephanie snarled at me shaking a flour covered finger at me. "You don't know Susanna Grace. That man was devastated. Ben and PJ watched him like a pair of hawks for weeks. They were terrified he would take a drink to drown the memories. He did nothing but support you in this."

"I could feel us slipping Steph," I admitted for the first time to anyone. "I was so busy. He was busy. Phone calls missed. Skype dates cancelled because of restaurant shifts or interviews. I was holding him back. Then we get into a fight no sooner than he got to Europe. We even argued the one night I did get to see him. So yes, I was a chicken and I ran. Tried to protect myself for the inevitable."

"Inevitable huh?" she drawled rolling her eyes sliding a bowl of dough to me to get started on. "Y'all have broken up before that. Known for keeping this whole town on edge to see how long it would take y'all to work it out because you always did. But this time, I'm not sure there is any coming back from it."

"There been anyone else?" I asked timidly not sure if I wanted to know the answer at all. Haunted me on the nights I couldn't sleep. Nights that I still woke up reaching for him even a year later. Leaving him sleeping in that hotel room was one of the hardest things I have ever done. My thoughts quickly flashed to the damn messages Katie Benson had sent me while I was gone. Damn bitch thrived on pissing me off. I didn't want to even believe what she had been insinuating. Something going on with B and Sadie. No chance in hell.

I knew he had gotten to be good friends with her especially after the final downfall of her and Luke. Glad she'd had him here since I had failed her in the ways she needed me. There was little smirks from customers when they came in. Quiet whispers that confused me. Like the whole damn town knew something I didn't. Stephanie smothered a laugh making me growl. "What?"

"Oh maybe a date or two," she chuckled then quickly shook her head with a quiet laugh. "You know Southern mama's and their meddling. That's all. Didn't amount to anything that I know of. Or that I have heard Ben mention. What about you? Or did you spend the rest of the time baking your ass off pining away for the outlaw you were stupid enough to let go?"

"Umm..." I said biting my bottom lip feeling my cheeks flare red as Steph's eyes blew wide. "There may have been someone."

"Who?" Stephanie gasped looking at me in surprise. "You barely were left with time to call home so when did you have time to date."

"Because it was Jacques," I spit out looking at my hands refusing to see the shock on my cousin's face. "It was a couple of wine fueled nights Steph. He's older so I let that spin my mind. Clouded my judgement."

"Please dear God tell me it was after you broke up with BG?" Stephanie snapped making my head fly up in shock. "I will beat your ass if it wasn't Susanna Grace!"

"It was," I yelled back seeing relief in her eyes. Guilt in mine. This time last year I was sure that I'd been looking into the eyes of the man I would spend the rest of my life with. That we would weather the storm of being apart a year. Throwing my hands up flour went everywhere. "I missed Brantley. We'd all been drinking one night and things just went that direction. I was single. Thought why the hell not. You can't sit here trying to tell me that if B had been in the same situation he wouldn't have acted too!"

Stephanie was about to say something else, but the back door of the bakery came open making us both freeze. Her face immediately softened from the hard lines it was set in towards me. Ben walked on with a backwards hat covering his trademark mohawk pulling his dark glasses off. His face lit up seeing Stephanie. He moved closer wrapping his long arms around her in a hug kissing her quickly. Spotting me, his normally friendly eyes narrowed for a half second before he sighed stepping around Steph.

"Come here Suzie Q," Ben chuckled holding his arms out. I gratefully walked into them feeling myself lifted in a bear hug. A soft kiss pressed to the top of my head. "Good to finally have you home."

"Thanks Ben," I murmured when he sat me back on my feet. I looked up at my cousin's boyfriend with tons of questions flooding my mind that I had no right to ask. Thankfully Stephanie interrupted me before I could. Just make a fool of myself anyways.

"You're back earlier than I thought you would be babe," Stephanie said as Ben nodded with a smile. "Not that I am complaining at all."

"Yea we got the video wrapped pretty quick," he chuckled. "Still think I am getting mud out of my ears. BJ divebombed me into one of the biggest mudholes in the whole damn park. PJ swore it was like herding kids. Should turn out badass. I leave again Tuesday since we are in the studio before hitting the road."

"Well then," Stephanie sighed playfully. "Guess I will have to enjoy the few days I have you home then."

"Go ahead and get out of here Steph," I said giving her a quick smile knowing it didn't quite meet my eyes. "I'll handle things here. Lord knows you have done enough for me. Spend time with Ben." Ben flashed me a toothy grin as Stephanie's jaw dropped. It hit me just how selfish I had been in depending on her for so much. I waved my hands as Stephanie untied her apron looking up at him. "Go on get out of here."

"Well I won't argue," Stephanie said walking over to hug me. Her first real one since I got back. "Call me if you need anything. And for heaven's sake don't make this place over with any more French stuff!" "Okay!" I laughed watching the pair of them walking out whispering to themselves. Regret pooled in my stomach. I'd had that. Or I did until stupidly walking away from it. If Ben was home that more than likely meant Brantley was. Laying low was sounding like a smart plan for me.

I stayed late after the bakery closed doing the rest of the prep for tomorrow. I finished typing out the text to Steph that it was covered as I walked into my quiet house. Biting my lip as I looked up, I sighed because it used to not be this quiet. On the rare nights I would stay at home I usually was greeted by the tv blaring. The clicking of claws on the hardwood floors tackling me coming through the door. But it was eerily silent. Making my way to my room I sighed at the pile of laundry waiting on me to hang it up. Putting my phone on the charger, I started putting it away keeping myself busy.

I prayed sleep claimed me early tonight. I was finally getting back on this time zone but still even after all these months sleeping alone got to me. Missed the warm arms wrapped around me at night. Hanging one of sundresses up, I caught sight of a t-shirt hanging with mine that gave me pause. I slipped the familiar faded black shirt off the hangar clutching it my chest. The scent I was wishing for long faded. Tears welled in my eyes. I couldn't do this to myself. Just end up eating me alive. I made my choice. I had to live with it and the memories that came with it. My phone vibrating on the nightstand pulled me from my misery. I sniffled reaching for it seeing a text from Mama.

Mama: Girl's night for margaritas Friday night. No is not an answer daughter of mine. Consider yourself summoned. Pick you up at six.

Well shit I thought with a groan. She'd tapped me for one of their margarita nights. So much for laying low. Those nights were so famous around here that even the preacher turned a blind eye to it. Pretty sure the bartender had been using LeClaire's special recipe for them for a while now. I would be lucky to leave there sober.

Well Susanna is home. Seems that she is different. Gonna find out all that has changed while she has been gone? Keep eyes peeled for an update here and how Sadie sees things from in Crash My Party. Wonder what BG will say when he finds out she is home....

Not A Warm Welcome: Part II

Mama Becky's POV

I leaned back in my seat of Connie's SUV watching Susanna and Sadie both staring out the windows not talking to each other. Stephanie playing middle man between the two. LeClaire had claimed shotgun before we ever left my house with Kolby at the wheel playing our chauffer for the night. Even the preacher turned a blind eye to our margarita nights. Sadly the sheriff too after that one time we left with the sombreros holding each other up singing "Jose Curveo You Are A Friend of Mine". We were added to part of the infamy of Jackson County.LeClaire swore that she was going to get his wife to participate one night.

I chuckled to myself thinking about Luke leaning against the doorway holding Bo when Sadie climbed in. Oh if looks could have killed over the shorts she was wearing. Then you had Susanna in at least a more casual version of herself than I had seen since she came home. The black chiffon dress draped down showing off tan shoulders with a fair amount of tan leg with stacked heel black strappy sandals. Know my youngest pulled his shades down when she walked out.

No doubt my oldest son would have just backed her back into the house. When Connie had called to tell me Susanna was due home I had hung up worried. Yes, I knew what the rumors flying around town about Brantley and Sadie were. Knew something had happened at least once but according to Kolby that had been it. Even Connie had shocked me in her nonchalance over it. Her exact words had been no one should expect Brantley to wait around forever.

Reaching the restaurant, I climbed out but paused waiting on the girls to clamor out of the back. I laid a hand on Susanna's arm before she could get away. Unsure amber pools stared back at me when she turned fully facing me. Bit her red painted bottom lip studying me. I got a surprised gasp when I tugged her to me in a hug. Did my heart good to realize she still smelled like vanilla cupcakes. At least that hadn't changed. Felt her relax against me returning it with a quiet sigh. Pulling back, I cupped her cheek. Hated the misery and heartache she thought she was hiding in her eyes. Bless her if she was like this and hadn't even seen Brantley yet. All I saw looking back at me was the look that had haunted his eyes for months.

"It's good to have you home honey," I told Susanna giving her a smile. I received a tentative one in return. "You've been missed."

"Thanks Ms. Becky," Susanna said quietly tucking a strand of chin length hair behind her ear. Short and sassy just like I knew she could be. I glared at her before she giggled. "Sorry Mama Becky. Wasn't sure...."

"Regardless of the situation," I reassured her with a smile. "I will always be that to you sweetheart. Now go find us a table."

I watched her follow Stephanie and Sadie inside before putting my hands on my hips raising an eyebrow at LeClaire who was strolling up as Connie paused doing the same thing. LeClaire rolled her eyes at both of us.

"What?" she rasped with a throaty chuckle. "You two are giving me a look. Why is that?"

"This hairbrained scheme to get the four of them talking again better work," I sighed knowing we had to be out of our minds. Luke and Sadie had two very good reasons to remain civil with each other. Brantley and Susanna on the other hand didn't. Why the four of them fought against it I will never know.

"I agree," Connie chuckled looking at me. "They need a push but not sure this is it. Lot of things left unsaid. Lot more still unknown for each of them."

"Answer me this," LeClaire asked taking the last drag of her cigarette before stubbing it out giving us both a smirk. "Do you two want grandkids before you are too old to enjoy them?"

"Yes," we both said. Kolby walked up swinging Connie's keys around with a laugh. LeClaire nodded her head with a broad smile.

"Well then let's get to drinking shall we," she laughed making me chuckle. Kolby shook his head.

"Yep," he muttered holding the door open for us. "There will be fireworks from all this for sure. A shit show is what is gonna happen."

Later on after the drinks and shots were flowing freely, I watched Susanna's tan skin grow more flushed. Eyes getting glassier. I excused myself to walk towards the bathroom. Lifting my phone up, I unlocked the screen pressing on Brantley's speed dial calling to make sure he was home. Keeping up my part in this master plan. Sure enough he was. Had been staying close to the house ever since getting back in town the other day to keep from running into Susanna with no doubt. Well, may have to change that.

Susanna's POV

I blinked my eyes feeling my mouth hang so low I bet my jaw had come unhinged. There was silence at our table and the next three over had whipped around in their seats. I swore if Mabel Jenkins leaned any further out of her chair she was going to face plant the floor. Or maybe that was me after the shots Stephanie kept sliding to me. Sadie and I had kept pace with each other on shots. Giggling and laughing like nothing had changed until the bomb she had just dropped.

Mama Becky approached the table with wide eyes seeing us being quiet. Except for Sadie who was calmly leaning back in her chair beside me with a cat ate the canary grin. Steph reached for my wrist pushing my hand to the tequila shot she had been trying to pass me. I know the woman who I had considered to be one of my best friends just did not admit to sleeping with Brantley. I threw the shot back without so much as a blink before a growl slipped past my lips

"What the hell did you just say Sadie Lynn?" I hissed leaning closer to her only to be yanked back by Stephanie trying to keep a grip on me. A slim arm had an almost death grip around my neck as I scrambled to get free. Mama's jaw was dropped seeing me trying to dive at my former best friend as my cousin tried her level best to keep me from swinging. "YOU SLEPT WITH BRANTLEY!!!"

"Sure did," Sadie chuckled thinking this was the funniest thing in the world. What it was actually doing was breaking my heart more than it already was. Regardless of the fact all this was my fault. "You heard what I said. Unless being in Europe effected your hearing." She leaned closer to me with a smirk. "That thing he does with his...."

"Shut the fuck up right now!" I snapped trying to free myself from Stephanie making me own my mama make the sign of the cross. Rage was quickly burning off the tequila flowing through my veins. Mama Becky stood frozen near the table her phone dangling from her fingers. LeClaire looked like she needed a huge bag of popcorn for the expected show. Her phone lit up at her elbow making me wonder who was texting her. Tears and rage burned in my eyes as Sadie's grin widened at my shock. I pointed a finger at her in disbelief. "I can't believe you! Broken up or not that was a line you should have never crossed!"

"Get off your damn high horse Suzie Q," Sadie snapped back pursing her lips at me. "You broke the man's heart. Did you expect him to wait around on you? Doubt you extended the same courtesy. Bet there was some French dude that rocked your world. How the hell you gave that up I will never know." Lips twisted up in an evil smile while Stephanie scrambled to keep me in my chair. I think she would force the whole bottle of tequila down my throat if it would keep me from killing Sadie. The teasing purr I heard next only inflamed my temper more. Sadie shook her hair back with an evil grin. "Ever call him Big Daddy during sex? My God the effect that has on that man..."

"Sweet Jesus," LeClaire whistled as Mama Becky turned as red as tomato and Mable Jenkins finally fell out of her chair. Hopefully her LifeAlert button was working. Mama turned her margarita up while Stephanie grabbed my cheeks putting the tequila bottle to my lips as I sputtered trying to think of a comeback. That fucking bitch was all I could think. What I heard next made me stop as LeClaire looked at her phone in relief. "Thank heavens Luke has made it to get the tipsy loudmouth over there."

Hearing the words that Luke was there had me pushing away from Stephanie climbing wobbly to my feet. I shot Sadie a grin of pure evil over my shoulder before stalking towards the front of the restaurant with only revenge on my mind. He may not completely be what I wanted but Mr. AssShaker and I needed to have a discussion. Might have to find out just how well he moved those hips somewhere other than on stage.

Brantley's POV

Out of the corner of my eye from my stretched out position on my garage floor I saw headlights sweep across the driveway. I frowned wondering just who the hell that was when everyone knew damn good and well I just wanted to be left alone. Then I remembered Kolby's text that he was dropping off something from Mama. Must be him. Knowing he could find me on his own, I fumbled around for the wrench I was looking for to finish tightening the screw on the motorcycle I was working on. Tried writing earlier but didn't work. So I had resorted to tinkering on my bikes to wear me out to the point of sleeping. Stopped myself a thousand times from taking a ride into Jefferson to just maybe catch a glimpse of Susanna. I growled at myself turning the wrench with a flex of my wrist just wishing I could forget about her. Nothing worked though. Only possibility was the one road I would not go down.

Determined clicking on the pavement made me still my movements. A second later black heels appeared near my head with blood red painted toenails peeping out. My eyes traveled up the tan legs I missed having wrapped around me. A swift kick to my shoulder had me growling up at the woman glaring down at me.

"What in the hell Susanna!" I yelled pushing out from underneath my bike sitting up glaring back. Hands on her slim hips. Even white teeth bared surrounded by ruby red lips. Her entire body was shaking with apparent rage as her purse kept trying to slip off her shoulder. Something had pissed her off and it seemed to be me for some reason. That and I could clearly see the alcohol haze to her eyes. "Why are you even here?"

"I can't believe you Brantley!" Susanna raged as I stared back at her. I felt my own temper flaring at the animosity that had been simmering for months. What the hell had I done? I heard my phone chime in my pocket as I stood up bowing my shoulders just a little. Don't think it didn't go unnoticed that Susanna's eyes widened when I did it. Raked them right over my bare chest down to the top of my jeans. This put my bike between the two of us which worried me a little. She had a tendency to throw things occasionally when mad at me. I may or may not have ducked a rolling pin a few times. Seeing her this close again after all these months made me ache to hold her.

Something was wrong and every instinct in me wanted to fix it. God, I had missed her with everything in me. Pissed me off that I hadn't been able to move on. Susanna's hands propped on her hips as she glared at me. If looks could kill I was as good as dead. As I was pulling my phone out reading the text, she finally told me what was wrong with her. "You fucking slept with Sadie! How could you! I'd rather you have banged Jana than to sleep with my best friend!"

Sadie: Warning! Warning! They know what happened!

I frowned down at my screen typing back a reply as Susanna got even more wound up.

B: No shit Sherlock! I am currently being screamed at. Figure she is two seconds away from throwing tools at my head. Call me if Luke gets too out of line.

"Are you fucking texting Sadie!" Susanna screamed making me jerk my head up with a snarl. She reached across the motorcycle smacking a slim hand into my chest. I ignored the sting as well as the jolt of her skin hitting mine.

"So what the fuck if I am!" I roared back throwing the wrench in my hand making a yelp slip out into the now quiet night before it pinged hitting the wall across from us. I shook my phone at her before slipping it in my pocket. "You left me remember! Like a damn thief in the night! Gave up the right to have any say in what I do!"

"Thief in the night huh," she taunted tapping her foot on the garage floor. "That's your term for it?"

"What the hell else am I supposed to say huh?" I roared back. All the anger, hurt, and loneliness that was brewing under the surface for months coming to a head. Tears shimmered in her amber eyes. "I woke up to an empty bed and a note. A FUCKING NOTE SUSANNA!!! I loved you! Saw myself spending the rest of my life with you and that is the stunt you pulled! Thought I meant more to you than that."

"Loved huh?" Susanna said with a sniffle shaking her head making her now shorter hair swing. My eyes trailed over her not quite sure to think of her look now. I had overheard Stephanie on the phone with Ben bitching about how much she had changed. "That's all you can say. Guess I shouldn't be surprised since you slept with Sadie."

"What the hell else do you want me to say!" I snapped throwing my hands up in defeat hearing a scoff slip past her lips. "Yes, I slept with Sadie okay. In a moment of loneliness and weakness for both of us. I just wanted to feel something other than like my heart had been ripped in two. It was just sex! We really are nothing more than good friends. Hell most days she is my best friend. Not that you can relate to needing that from anyone. Always so damn stubborn and independent."

"Actually," Susanna murmured barely above a whisper. Something akin to revenge twinkled in her eyes. "I probably could. Paris does get lonely after a few glasses of wine. Guess you aren't the only one who can have just sex." My hands balled into fists at her words feeling intense jealously swell through every fiber of my being. The thought of any other man's hands on her driving me insane. Seeing the look on my face Susanna stepped back with a sigh. "I really shouldn't be here. I'll go find my way home."

She turned heading to the doorway of the garage as I stood there fuming. I grabbed the closet tools nearing me throwing them as hard as I could one after another with a roar. Susanna paused at the door her shoulders set in a rigid line. I stalked after her kicking one of my helmets out of the way sending it flying past her making her yelp. So furious I could barely see straight.

"Who?" I seethed hearing my boots echo as I stomped closer to her. Susanna peered over a slim tan shoulder at me with wide eyes. A deep growl echoed all around us as my temper fully snapped. "Who dammit? I asked you a fucking question! That group partner of yours that had zero respect for you having a boyfriend? Some random guy in a bar? Fucking who Susanna!"

"Jacques," she said with a whimper rounding out into a gasp as my hand circled her arm yanking her around to face me. Gripping her tight but not tight enough to bruise. She swallowed deeply. "We had been drinking after closing and one thing led to another. It happened a couple of times. I was lonely. Had cut myself pretty much off from home after breaking up with you. It was like you said just wanted to feel something even it was for a night. But..."

"But what?" I hissed lowering my face close to hers getting a faint whiff of the tequila she surely had been drinking on tonight's girls' night. My lips an inch from hers as we glared at each other. "But what Susanna?"

"He wasn't you," she murmured pushing up on her tiptoes brushing her lips against mine. I froze feeling my entire body lock up at the brief contact. Susanna dropped back down to her feet looking up at me biting her lip. "I'm sorry. I shouldn't have done that."

"You're probably right," I snapped as she yanked her arm free from my hand backing away from me. What were either us thinking right now? Anger I knew for sure. Perhaps....

Welllll the cat is out of the bag on that one night tryst. To see how Sadie spilled the beans and Luke's thoughts flip on over to Crash My Party to find out. Meanwhile we shall be in the tepee....

Consequential Reveals

Susanna's POV

I took a couple shaky steps cursing Stephanie under my breath for all the tequila. Mad at Mama for coercing me into going out tonight. As soon as I stopped seeing double of everything I was gonna punch Kolby straight in the mouth for dropping me off at Brantley's. This was not the place I needed to be after what I found out tonight. The evil gleam that had been in Sadie's eyes wounded me more than anything. I knew I had turned out to be a shitty friend but still.

Stumbling over my drunken feet along with the heels I was wearing I fell forward knowing I was about to kiss the concrete. A long arm slipped around my waist pulling me up from certain doom. Green eyes narrowed down at me as I was turned to face him. The sober side of Susanna tried to convince the drunk side to hold her ground and not stare at the bare tattooed chest an inch from her nose. Well let's just say drunk Susanna was winning.

"You been drinking tonight?" Brantley asked me gruffly making my head snap up with a glare. So what the hell if I have. I received a warning growl for my glare. Yea well fuck him too. Right now everyone could kiss my ass because sure they all knew about those two doing the mattress mambo. Lord, I looked like a fool I am sure. Nothing was kept quiet in this small town. "I asked you a question Susanna Grace."

"Maybe I have," I purred stepping closer eliminating all space between us seeing him inhale deeply as I wrapped my arms around his neck teasing my nails along his shoulders. I shook my hair out of my face pushing up on my tiptoes again hovering my lips over his before sinking my teeth into Brantley's bottom lip. "We both know tequila makes me frisky and my clothes fall off. How about we take this upstairs?"

"No," Brantley murmured shaking his head slowly. I kept in the whimper of despair that wanted to slip out. Did he not know how much I missed him? How sorry I was for what I did? Being this close was driving me insane even as things were growing fuzzier. I tried again only to be gently pushed back making my eyes well with tears. "I can't Susanna."

"Of course you can't," I hissed putting both my hands in the middle of his chest shoving him back. "I'm not Sadie! Hell, I never could even compare to anyone else so let's just add her to the list! I fucked up okay! That what you want to hear?"

"Tonight is not the night for this," he sighed as I stalked around him pacing the garage not looking at him. I put my back to him bracing my hands on the table near his toolbox drumming my fingers on it willing the tears not to fall. "We are both pissed. You are drunk.."

"What that your plan all along?" I asked not even looking back. "To get with Sadie. Why you stepped up to help so much after Luke cheated on her in Mexico? After she found out she was pregnant and I wasn't here to help like I should?"

"Seriously Susanna Grace!" Brantley snapped as I idly stroked my fingers over the wrench in front of me. "Guess your next question will be if Bo is mine or not?"

"Well it did cross my mind!" I hissed back gripping the wrench so tight my knuckles turned white. "I mean you were glued to her side anytime you were home from what I heard."

"Unfuckingbelievable!" he roared kicking a stack of boxes near him. "There anything else you want to question! Because for the record Bo is Luke's. No doubt in anyone's mind on that! Next...."

"Was she better than me?" I snapped out knowing this was the tequila talking. But it was eating at me. I turned my head to see his reaction. What I saw was the widest, most evil shit eating grin I had ever seen the man wear in all the years I'd known him. And he could be a cocky son of a bitch when he wanted to. My temper fully snapped then as I raised my hand hurling the wrench in my hand with everything ounce of anger I was feeling behind it.

Fate must have been on my side because it nailed my intended target right in the forehead with a heavy thud. Brantley let out a yell as my jaw dropped. The wrench clanged to the floor. He reached up pressing fingers to his forehead coming back with a trace of blood glaring at me. Holding his head with one hand and stalking towards me, my arm was grabbed roughly pushing me towards the door leading to the kitchen.

"That's fucking it!" Brantley roared keeping an iron grip on my arm dragging me through the house. "I ought to turn that ass of your bright red right now! But I don't even want to look at you." He pushed me down on the couch shaking a long finger at me. I felt sorta bad at the trickle of blood seeping down his cheek. Asshole asked for it though. "Stay put. I'm going to clean this up then I'm taking your drunk demented ass home." He turned to stalk away as I let out a huff. I had shifted to stand lifting one ass cheek off the couch when he yelled again. "I mean it! Don't fucking move!"

"Bossy ass," I murmured to myself crossing my arms over my chest. I looked around the room noting nothing had changed since I left other than a few pictures missing. Ones that had me in them. Guess he really had written me off. A tear slipped down my cheek as a sob bubbled up. I brought this on myself. I left. Then I ended things because I was terrified of getting hurt. Kicking my sandals off, I laid down on my side with the intent of resting my eyes for a few moments to regroup before having to face the irate Brantley that would come thundering downstairs soon.

Next thing I knew sunlight was filtering in making me blink. That along with the buzzing of my phone made my aching head pound as I pried my eyes open. I had the headache from hell, my mouth felt like the Sahara Desert and I couldn't figure out why I was sleeping on my couch. The low snore near me made me realize this wasn't my couch. Sitting up slowly holding my head, I glanced over at Brantley sleeping in his chair. A set of white butterfly band aids gracing his forehead. Shit, I thought with a wince. I really did throw something at him last night. My phone buzzing again from the coffee table had me reaching for it idly unlocking the screen.

Mama: Big Daddy?? Really son! I could have gone the rest of my life without hearing that! Hope you enjoyed the gift your brother dropped off.

Shit! Soooo not my phone. I chanced a look over at Brantley seeing him still passed out. Why he slept down here instead of in his room I dunno. Unable to help it, I opened up another message. I growled reading it.

Julie: Hey handsome! Ran into your sweet mama the other day at the grocery store. Call me if you have some time off. Maybe go on that third date?

For fucks sakes even his mama had been trying to set him up after I broke up with him. The last one made my already steaming blood pressure rise which resulted in my head pounding harder. I thought I was gonna be sick.

Sadie: Checking to make sure you were still alive. Please tell me you at least got Susanna home safely without any bloodshed. Luke was pretty pissed.

"If you are done going through my phone," I heard growled making me drop the phone with a guilt yelp. I turned my head seeing Brantley lowering the footrest of his recliner glaring at me sleepily. "Guess I can take you home now."

"That you were last night," I mumbled ducking my head in defeat. He didn't leave me down here by myself. Why I had no clue. "I didn't mean to fall asleep."

"With all the tequila running through your veins it is no wonder," he sighed standing up stretching his arms over his head. Ever had exactly what you wanted standing right in front of you but was in truth a million miles away. How I felt right now. Tired, sad eyes studied me as he stepped closer leaning down to grab his phone. The desire to bury my fingers in the soft t-shirt yanking him down to the couch beside me was so strong I had to bite my lip to stop myself. A big hand reached out to gently pull me to my feet. "Let me take you home and you can finish sleeping the drama of last night off."

Mid July 2016

Brantley's POV

The early morning hours were the worst when I couldn't sleep. Songwriting for the new album had at least helped give me an outlet for all that was going on in my life. No matter what I did I couldn't get Susanna out of my head. Months ago it was easier in some ways because of out of sight out of mind. After the night out fiasco, all the quiet whispers had gotten louder around home. Couldn't even stand the thought of passing that white Jeep driving through town. I stayed gone. Took every writing session I could. Hide in the studio when the opportunity was there. Mama had yelled at me for ten minutes the other day for not coming home to face things.

Moving on was the smart thing to do. Finding out about her and that French fucker coupled with the revelation of my one night with Sadie was the final nail in the coffin of anything being rekindled between Susanna and I. How could either of us get over the jealousy that had been sparked out of searching for a cure for our loneliness? That's even if she had been lonely. I sighed rubbing a hand over my face wishing I had loaded the bike up for this leg so I could go for a ride to clear my head. Stuck is what I was in so many ways. I'd sat there watching her sleep for hours that night. Aching to curl up with her in my arms just too damn stubborn to take that chance. Too afraid of getting hurt again. I was better off keeping my walls up.

Overheard Stephanie, who was with us for the weekend, telling PJ earlier than Susanna was working herself to the bone these past few weeks. I'd received a glare from each of them like this was my damn fault. Umm....no it wasn't. I didn't get drunk and broadcast something that should have been in front of half the town. I didn't show up at my house ranting and raving about it. Admitting defeat, I pushed up from the couch with the intent to pad to the back. Hopefully sleep wouldn't evade me tonight. I'd taken a couple steps when a pounding knock sounded on the bus door. I whirled around with a growl stalking there to fling it open with a snarl. I drew up short when a teary eyed frantic Stephanie rushed at me.

"B," she whimpered throwing her arms around me as I settled mine around her in shock. Ben stepped up behind her with tears in his eyes and pale faced. Big hands rested on Steph's shoulders as I wondered what the hell was going on. Stephanie lifted her head wiping at her face. "Brantley. We have got to get home. Like right now."

Yes I know....woman you are in trouble. I was already in the teepee anyw
ays.......

Finding Home Again

B rantley's POV

I shot my baby brother a grateful look as his truck stopped in the driveway. Jumping out of the truck, I hurried up the walkway right as the first rays of sun were slipping over the horizon. About the time I bent over to fish out the spare key from under the flower pot, the door swung open revealing a teary eyed Tiffany. The look of utter grief and relief in her eyes made my heart stop. She stepped to the side letting me into the house shutting the door behind us. Before I could open my mouth she reached a hand over squeezing my arm.

"Thank God you are here B," She murmured wiping a tired hand over her face. "You were the first thing she asked for once the shock settled in."

"Where is she?" I asked softly praying maybe she was getting some sleep. Tiffany jerked her head towards the hall. I headed that way with determined steps easing the cracked door open. The shaking lump in the middle of the bed broke my heart. I looked back at Tiffany with a nod before closing the door. Kicking my shoes off as I walked, I crawled onto the bed feeling my eyes well with tears at the quiet whimpering sobs. I stretched out after laying my phone and hat to the side before gently pulling the comforter back. Tousled auburn hair and bloodshot amber eyes peered back at me.

"Hey baby girl," I said pushing Susanna's hair away from her face hearing a whimper while a fresh round of tears slipped down her cheeks. Holding my arms open, she burrowed her face into my chest. Smoothing gentle hands along her back I felt tears soaking my t-shirt. I pressed a comforting kiss to the top of her head. "Let it all out sweetheart. I'm here."

"I can't believe she's gone," Susanna sobbed brokenly. "Please tell me it is a dream B."

"I would if I could baby. Oh how I wish it was all a dream," I sighed shifting with her in my arms. The harder she cried the tighter I held her. Deep gut wrenching sobs. At one point she lost her breath. "Susanna honey, you've got to calm down."

Slim fingers twisted into my t-shirt clinging for dear life. Once Stephanie had calmed down long enough to explain to me what happened PJ had driven us to the airport for the first flight out. I was glad we had gotten here as soon as we did. I nervously drummed my fingers the whole flight worried about what state Susanna would be in once we got home. Stephanie had finally cried herself to sleep on Ben's shoulder. A grim faced Kolby had greeted us at the airport.

Holding Susanna, I couldn't even imagine what Coach Hale was feeling at the moment. Mrs. Connie was a staple of this town that was irreplaceable. Always a smile on her face with a kind word for everyone. First to put all the past and present football and baseball teams in their places if they needed to be. Was hard to hear that a deer had caused her to swerve coming home from her book club meeting making her overcorrect. She was a lady in this town that would sorely be missed.

Quiet voices in the hall pricked my ears wondering who Tiffany was talking to. I hadn't even known she was still here. A second later the door cracked open. My eyes widened slightly seeing Sadie walk in. Concern echoing in the depths of her blue eyes. She drew up short for a second noticing that Susanna was curled around me before nodding and stepping in the room. I could feel the apprehension from her wondering how Susanna would react to her presence.

But she was so far gone in her grief that it wasn't registering. Sadie walked around to the other side of the bed sitting down with a tired smile. Looked like she hadn't gotten much sleep. Knew from what little she had told me Luke was giving her some space right now. She laid a soft hand on Susanna's arm making her turn her head on my chest blinking in the dim light.

"Hey Suzie Q," Sadie said quietly. A quiet sniffle was her answer as I sat up slowly putting my back against the headboard then shifted Susanna up into my lap. Her head immediately tucked into the crook of my neck while she stretched her legs out on mine meeting Sadie's eyes. All of the animosity between them was at a stand still when Susanna tentatively reached a hand out for Sadie's searching for that link. "Sweetie I don't have any words to say and help. But..." She reached into the pocket of her shorts pulling out an alcohol swab and a syringe holding it up. "I do have this. B, it's a sedative. Daddy figured she could use something after hearing the news. There is a prescription for some sleeping pills on the counter. Make sure Steph gets them filled for her."

Susanna whimpered nodding her head burrowing closer as Sadie shifted pushing up her shirt sleeve to give her the shot. Nails dug into my arm while the needle pricked her skin then relenting once Sadie was finished. Surprise registered on Sadie's face when Susanna sat up reaching over to hug her. Tears welled in Sadie's eyes when she met mine over Susanna's shoulder. She pulled back cupping Susanna's cheek with a watery smile. "You get some rest. I'm only a phone call away if you need me."

I nodded as Susanna stretched out beside me before reaching for my arm. Shifting behind her, I wrapped both arms around her tight feeling her slim fingers wrapping around mine. Legs tangled as her breathing started to even out lulling me to sleep as well. After all the sleepless nights without her I hated it took something like this for her to be curled up with me again. Burying my face into the curve of my neck I let the quiet pull me under with her. I knew the next few days would be rough.

Hours later a low moan dragged me from the edges of deep sleep feeling Susanna jolt in my arms. Her whole body going stiff as I came awake. Thinking she needed to get up, I untangled my arms and legs from her letting her ease off the bed. Pushing disheveled hair away from her face, she glanced at the time realizing it was early afternoon then looked back down at me as I stretched sitting up. Susanna looked down at her feet biting her lip then back up at me. Her face completely locked down. Shit. This was not going to be good. Arms crossed sinking into herself as she looked at me.

"You can go Brantley," she murmured with harsh undertones to her voice. "I've got a lot to take care of."

"Alright," I said running a hand over my face yawning before swinging my feet to the floor. "Where do we start?"

"We?" Susanna snapped shaking her head. There she went locking it down and pushing me away. "There is no we. I didn't even know...."

"You stop it right there," I warned lowly before slipping on my shoes glaring at her. "Like hell you are about to push me away right now. You need me Susanna."

"I'll be fine on my own," she sighed shaking her head. "I have to keep it together to stay strong for Daddy. It's what.."

"And what about you?" I asked watching her pace around her room straightening idle things to avoid the subject. Always so damn stubborn. Thinking she always has to do things on her own. I walked over trying to put my arms around her only to have both hands put in the middle of my chest pushing me away. I glared baring my teeth at her. "Fine. That's the way you want it huh. Gonna tell me I came rushing home for nothing."

"If that's what you want to think then fine," Susanna growled shoving me again. I tried to reign my temper in reminding myself this was the pain and grief talking. "I didn't ask you to! Sorry for taking up your time!"

"Damn stubborn ass!" I snapped shaking a finger at her. I stomped over grabbing my hat and phone praying that Kolby had dropped my truck off if not I would be calling for a ride. I wrenched the bedroom door open walking out. "Have it your way!"

A surprised Tiffany jerked up on the loveseat as I stalked through the living room. Ben lifted his head from where he was laying on the couch with a passed out Stephanie on his chest. He sighed then pointed at the coffee table. I stalked over grabbing my keys before turning on my heel to walk away. No doubt the two of them had heard it all. Climbing in my truck I backed out of the driveway trying to not squeal my tires giving Susanna's neighbors anymore to talk about. We'd been the town gossip enough here lately.

Reaching the end of her street, I paused slamming my hands down on the steering wheel with a frustrated yell. Then I narrowed my eyes. Fuck this. She didn't get a choice. Pushing me away when I know she needed someone for when she broke was not an option. Even if I had to turn her ass red for trying. I was taking the choice out of her hands knowing she needed me. I quickly turned around pulling back into Susanna's driveway. Maybe

I could coax her into coming out to the house away from so many prying eyes in town. Give her some peace of mind on that at least. I climbed out jogging back to the front door pulling it open.

Tiffany let out a laugh at seeing me again noting the determined look on my face. Flinging the bedroom door open, I opened my mouth poised to let Susanna really have it but stopped. What I found instead of her standing there fuming that I was back was her curled up on the bed with the pillow I had been sleeping on clutched in her arms like a life preserver. Stepping over to the bed, I sat down smoothing her hair away from her face idly stroking my thumb over her cheek wiping at the tears. She sniffled shamefully meeting my eyes.

"Let me tell you something Susanna Grace," I murmured seeing her eyes widen. "I'm not going anywhere. Push me away. Fight me. Scream and yell. I'm still going to be right here. You are not going through this alone do you hear me? Not happening baby girl. Whatever you need I am right here. I didn't haul ass home worried sick about you for no reason. Understand me?" Susanna bit her bottom lip nodding her head. "Good." I slipped an arm underneath her pulling her up against my chest. "Let's get something to eat in you even though I am sure you don't want anything. Then we can go from there okay."

"Okay," Susanna sniffled letting me stand up easing her to her feet. Fingers laced with mine as I led her to the door. She paused at the doorway looking up at me with sad eyes. A deep mournful sigh puffed out of her lips. Chin wobbled with another round of unshed tears. "Thank you B. I know you had to drop..."

"Suz," I said with a humorless chuckle guiding her down the hall pressing a kiss to the top of her head. "Haven't you figured out by now there is not much I won't do for you? Being here for you is more important okay."

I got a quick nod feeling her relax into my side approaching everyone in the living room. She was going to need all of us to make it through the next few days and the months to come. Just prayed I could will her enough strength for it all.

Rough few days ahead. Keep an eye out for Luke's POV of this duo coming soon in Crash My Party

Really Gone

Susanna's POV

Stepping through the doors of the funeral home turned my stomach like the clinging scent of death under all the flowery smell was crawling all over me. I paused greeting a great aunt who lived five states away biting the inside of my cheek to keep from gagging at the smell of her perfume. She rambled on about how she couldn't believe I was so much older now while I prayed she didn't pinch my cheek. For crying out loud woman I was twenty-eight not five. I might just deck her if she did.

My parent's house earlier had been descended on by the age old Southern tradition for grief, food. One thing for sure in a small town like this you lost a family member, you were well fed. Ben had remarked earlier he thought all the fried chicken in Jefferson was in the house. Fingers lacing with mine made said great aunt gasp at who was near my side as I quietly excused myself knowing it was time. Yea, yea Aunt Gertrude that is who you thought it was. Time to see the one thing I never wanted to see. My own mama laying in what amounted to a decorated box. Step by step closer to the chapel doors at the funeral home, I felt my body tremble as tears that I thought had long been cried out bubbled to the surface.

"I can't B," I murmured looking up at Brantley in despair. The tender concern reflected there almost sent me to my knees. I didn't deserve any of the support he was giving me. "I can't go in there."

"Then we go outside," he answered quietly lowering his head near mine. The top of my head disappearing under his black hat as he pressed his forehead to mine. Like he was surrounding me in a cocoon to block out all the questioning eyes in the room. It was like a cease gossip had happened in this town. But the wondering would start back up again once things were said and done. Wonder if the bets of are they or aren't they together would be whispered over coffee at the hardware store come Monday morning. "We do whatever you need to do. But baby, as rough as this is sure to be you have to face it."

"I know," I whimpered just wanting to escape anywhere but here. Turning my face towards the front the shocking amount of flowers took my breath away. I made a mental note to donate a majority to the local nursing homes praying the potted ones brought a smile to some faces. The arrangements that weren't real could be stored for later use. Daddy stood rigidly at the front of the aisle with his back to us not moving. Hands shoved into the pockets of the slacks he was wearing. I'd seen him break just once and it been enough to send me close to the edge of my sanity.

Timid step by step closer I eased forward. Brantley's grip on me never loosening as we walked. But as we got near the casket, my legs buckled. The arm around my waist held me up as my fingers turned white from gripping the hand holding mine. Flight instinct was kicking in even though I couldn't give in to it. Ripped my heart to see my mama, my own mama who had always seemed larger than life laying there just so damn still. I wondered if I cocked a sassy attitude would she sit up to ear tug me. Be strong Susanna is what I kept chanting in my head. Granny Hale walked by pressing a tissue to her eyes making her way to Daddy.

"I've got you," Brantley whispered his lips brushing my ear. His grip on me never wavering as we stepped closer. Tears streamed down my face, but I couldn't bring myself getting any closer. An arm slipped through mine as Stephanie stepped even with me sniffling lowly. I glanced over at her seeing Ben shifting his hold on her. Giving Brantley an absent nod, I let him guide me forward. From there things just went fuzzy as I felt like I was in a dream. Surely I was going to wake up. By the time things finally wound down I was convinced the entire town had passed through tonight. Sadie had pushed through a group of girls from high school that I really didn't even want to talk to. A raised eyebrow from her had sent them scurrying and Brantley smothering a laugh.

They both knew even with a word being spoken I was about to crawl out of my skin. A hard hug from her brought tears to my eyes even if I couldn't feel anything right now. Everything between us was irrelevant now. A quiet whisper in my ear to call if I needed anything had me nodding absently. I just wanted the quiet. Maybe a little bit in the dark just to forget things. Finally everyone was gone. An arm wrapped tightly around my waist guiding me out into the humid Georgia night air. Stephanie and Ben falling into step with us heading to the vehicles. Brantley stopped lifting a hand up to cup my face. "Where do you want to go?"

"Away," I whispered so lowly could barely be heard. Millions of miles away if I could. Part of me still as if I was dreaming. "But I need..."

"I'll stop by the house to get your stuff," he murmured opening the truck door for me helping me slide in. He turned speaking to Ben as I settled into the middle toying with the edge of my black skirt. Felt like I was underwater hearing things when he shut the door starting his truck. Big hand settling onto my knee. I whimpered at the simple gesture turning to bury my face in his shoulder listening to the radio playing quietly. Of all things to be playing Luke's "Drink A Beer" had to come on. Brantley lifted his hand to change it but I stopped him by lacing my fingers with his. We drove the rest of the way in silence.

Pulling into my driveway, I passed him my keys from my purse letting him jog towards the house to grab the bag packed with what I would need. Had stopped by on the way to the funeral home earlier but left it unsure where I would stay tonight. I couldn't be in my house alone unlike Daddy who was insisting on it. I looked up seeing Brantley coming back out of the house in the glow of the headlights.

My Jeep in its spot not moving at all this week. My dress for tomorrow held over his shoulder with my bag in his free hand. A moment later he climbed back in the driver's seat backing out pointing his truck towards Maysville. We passed the drive in silence. I followed into the house immediately heading for the stairs desperate to get out of this skirt and heels.

A quiet whine at the top of the stairs had a chuckle slipping past my lips. I leaned down as I got to the top pressing a kiss to the top of Sylo's head. He followed me towards Brantley's room as I walked to the closet in search of a t-shirt quickly changing into it. I hadn't even bothered with make up tonight knowing it would be no point in it. I sighed pinching the bridge of my nose against the headache as I crawled onto the big bed heading straight for the middle.

Burrowing under the covers shivering even if it was mid-July. Felt my canine protector lay his head on my hip snuggling close. The numbness flowing through me should scare me, but I welcomed it. Better than the incessant flow of tears. I didn't want to think about all she would miss from here on out. The most disturbing thought was the guilt. I heard footsteps but I never pulled the covers back to see what Brantley was doing. I was so mentally exhausted. If I was honest with myself, it was the days to come that scared me more than tomorrow did. Trying to figure out how to live my life with the noticeably heavy absences in it.

Brantley being so caring would surely not last once this was over. Could I really expect Sadie's concern to continue after I wasn't there for her when she needed me the most? Not sure how long it was before I felt the bed dip, the covers gently pulled away from my face. I puffed out a disgruntled sigh at my cocoon being disturbed. A soft chuckle sounded through the quiet of the room.

Bright full moon casting its light silhouetting the concerned features of the man stretching out beside me. Long fingers lifting to brush the hair away from my face. My heart ached at the tenderness in those green eyes I didn't deserve. God how much I had missed him this past year. If he just knew. But he wouldn't believe me now even if I told him after all that had happened. A rough thumb smoothed under my eyes.

"I know your exhausted sweetheart," Brantley said gently. Arms opened pulling me close. I sniffled burying my face into his neck wanting to hide from it all. Needed a time machine so I could go back telling Jacques no. The completely ostentatious floral arrangement in the corner had been from him. In a lot of ways, I hoped B hadn't seen it. The drama between us was at a standstill. But for how long. I tangled my legs with his, so I was completely surrounded. I pressed a soft kiss to the top of his chest out of habit as he played with the ends of my short hair. "What do you need baby?"

"You're doing it," I whispered lifting my head to meet his eyes. I leaned in brushing my lips against his taking in the comfort at the flip of my heart that familiar spark was still there. I laid my head back down closing my eyes. "Just by being you even if I don't deserve it."

"Not going through this alone Susanna," he whispered as I felt the dredges of exhaustion taking over. "I'll always be here for you."

Question is, I thought as I sank into oblivion, would he really always be?

For Sadie's view on how all this is going tune on into Crash My Party soon...

What Am I Gonna Do With You?

B rantley's POV

Shoving my hands into my pockets, I kept my eyes locked on the shaking figure ten feet in front of me standing guard. Luke squeezed my shoulder as he passed leading a sniffling Sadie towards his truck. I watched Coach step closer wrapping an arm around Susanna's trembling form resting his head against hers. Heard the distant boom of thunder knowing the late summer storm that had been threatening was looming closer and closer. Guess a good thunderstorm would help wash away some of the sorrow looming over this town.

Leaving next week was going to be hard. I knew I would worry the entire time. Already knew was no way I'd be able to talk her into going with us. She had already pushed Stephanie to go. Looking back over his shoulder, Coach motioned his hand for me to walk closer. I eased up meeting his worried eyes over the top of Susanna's head.

The tears in his eyes along with the sad smile made my heart ache more. I knew what he was about to say because he had called me this morning but Susanna didn't know that he was leaving tonight for a few weeks. I could understand why. Said he needed to get away to clear his head before football and school started.

"Son," Coach said gruffly clearing his throat. He turned Susanna in his arms to face him glancing at me. "Take care of her okay." I nodded my head quickly. He knew I meant it. He cupped Susanna's cheeks as she sniffled. "I'm gonna get away for a bit pumpkin. Take a road trip me and your mama had planned."

"But Daddy," Susanna sighed then jumped as the sound of thunder grew closer. I laid a hand on her arm hearing her sigh in defeat. He pressed a kiss to the top of her head. "Okay. Check in with me please."

I slipped an arm around her waist leading her to my truck where Ben was waited to hand off my keys. I took them and turned to open the door. Susanna hugged Ben tightly then climbed in. Stephanie gave me a small wave from the backseat of her daddy's truck. Climbing in my truck, I looked over at Susanna laying her head on the passenger window. Eyes closed securely. She had awake before I was this morning baking away. A full breakfast waiting when I came downstairs looking for her that I had only seen her take a bite or two of. She must have text Kolby because wasn't long after he came strolling in to fix a plate.

"Hey," I said softly as I drove out of town. She turned with teary eyes greeting me. "Why do we go change and drive into Atlanta to that hole in the wall Italian place you love."

"I'd like that," Susanna murmured quietly as a ghost of a smile came across her lips. "Think the last time I was there was...."

"Was when I took you for your birthday last year," I finished for her. An idea popped in my head as I turned down Main Street. "Why don't we make a night of it? If you feel up to it. We can get a room there. Get away for a little bit. Know you and Steph have the bakeries closed for the rest of the week. I've got to leave again Monday."

"Okay," Susanna said nodding. She bit her lip before pointing for the turn off for her street. "I need to go grab some clothes."

"Tiff put you a bag in here earlier," I explained as her eyes widened. She turned seeing it while I reached for her hand pulling her closer to me. My hand rested on her thigh where her dress had ridden up. "I'd like you to out at the house until then. Least I can make sure you sleep."

"As long as we take the Cougar tonight," she said with a laugh making me chuckle. I faked shock. "Yes B. I know you have it back from the shop."

Susanna's POV

After the mad rush of the morning, I retreated to the kitchen to work on prep. Stephanie was in Athens today training a couple new hires. The radio played lowly on the local country station. Steph had outlawed the "French shit" as she called it. I hummed along with Carrie thinking about the order she'd called me about for her son's birthday. Brantley left Monday morning for a couple of rescheduled interviews before tour dates for the week. The days following the funeral had been honestly spent in a bubble. We'd gone to dinner along with staying the night in Atlanta.

A few too many glasses of wine with dinner, I had found the courage to ask for what I wanted. Had desperately needed that connection to the man I loved but had stubbornly lost. Stirring awake in his arms the next morning with nothing between us but sheets and skin. Felt like heaven until the weight of why he was next to me settled in my chest. Losing my mama was the only reason Brantley was being kind to me after all I put him through.

The back door opening jerked my head from the cake I was working on. Sadie stepped in hesitantly chewing on her bottom lip. Her blue eyes glanced around probably judging which sharp kitchen instruments were closest to me. I gave her a tired smile motioning her inside. I knew the whole town had been patiently waiting on a cat fight between us. Resignation and numbness was what I felt in my chest over it all now. Also, life was too short. I gave her a quick grin pointing at the stool near me.

"I know I'm probably the last person you want to see right now," Sadie said quietly. I passed her a tray of iced sugar cookies. "But...."

"Sadie Lynn," I sighed ruefully making my hair swing as I shook my head. "Yes, you slept with B. We were split up. I did that. That was on me. But I also wasn't here when you needed me the most. I missed Bo coming into this world. If the last week or so has taught me anything it is that life is too short for grudges okay. Far as I am concerned it is water under the bridge. I know you love Luke."

"Just like that?" Sadie asked grabbing a sugar cookie raising an eyebrow. I winked reaching for the icing bag I needed. She nodded taking a bite reaching into her scrub pocket. Puffing out a sigh, she slid what was in her hand over to me. I gasped dropping the icing see the birthstone bracelet that looked like angel wings Daddy gave Mama a few Christmases ago that she always wore. We had assumed it had been lost in the car wreck. Tears streamed down my cheeks as I gingerly picked it up. "I found it in the hospital room that night. Knew you would want it. Just now found time to get it to you."

"Thank you," I whimpered wiping at my cheeks. I rounded the counter enveloping Sadie in a fierce hug. She hugged me tight as all the anger we'd felt for each other melted away. I heard my phone ringing on the counter but ignored it knowing it was early enough in the day I could call Brantley back. If she just knew how much I had missed her. I didn't deserve all of them being there for me.

"Of course," Sadie giggled as my phone rang again when I pulled back. Both of us wiping at our eyes. I was so tired of crying. Her phone chimed in her pocket making her sigh. "BG is calling you and there will be Mama wanting to know when I am coming for the kids."

"I understand," I smiled shaking my head. "He will worry even more if I don't answer soon. Why don't you drop Ryleigh off tomorrow to hang with me and Steph? I'll teach her how to make those scones since you love them."

"Finally over my aversion to blueberry," she said with a shudder making me grin. She waved as she headed to the door. "I'll text you later for a good time to drop her off."

Hearing the door close behind her, I slumped against the counter staring at the bracelet in my hand. She always wore it. The clasp had been fixed twice to make sure it was secure. Studying it, looked like it had broken again. I slipped it in my pocket biting my lip walking into my office. I reached in the desk draw pulling out the bottle of wine hidden in there. I was out of the sleeping pills Doctor Collins prescribed me. I'd barely slept the last few nights without a few glasses to numb the deep agonizes ache that hit when I was all alone.

But Daddy was still on his trip. Stephanie and I were busy with orders. Tiffany had used up enough vacation time lately for all that was going on. Sadie was working and had the kids. Brantley was back on the road. Everyone had their lives to live while I felt like I was spinning my wheels in a never ending circle of grief. I was drowning with no words to say. So a couple glasses did the trick. Surely one right now wouldn't hurt?

October 2016

Brantley's POV

I slammed my truck door so hard pretty sure Mama heard it five miles away. Pissed. Worried. Scared. You name it I was feeling it right now. I thought back to my conversation with Sadie on her way home to Tennessee earlier.

Still felt weird to think of her living there but she was happy. Stomping up the walkway I turned the knob for the front door growling when I found it locked. I yanked my keys out searching for the one I needed opening the door shutting it behind me.

I walked into the quiet house hearing just the faint sound of the television in the living room. My boots made hardly a sound on the hardwood floors as I spotted my quarry curled up in a ball hugging a pillow to her chest. My blood pressure went through the roof at the empty wine bottle and half full glass on the coffee table. I crossed my arms watching a slim hand reach out for it.

"SUSANNA GRACE HALE!" I roared making her sit up straight with a yell tumbling off the couch. She pushed up glaring at me with glassy eyes. Fuck. I was hoping she wasn't drunk but seemed she was. Her jaw dropped as I growled at her lowly before bracing my hands on the back of her couch. "Want to fucking explain last night?"

"I hung out with Sadie," she said nonchalantly the slight slur to her voice setting my teeth on edge. I glared harder at her. "What that's all it was! I needed a fun night out with my friend! Didn't realize that was a crime. What crawled up your ass? Also, why are you back in town? Thought you weren't home until next week."

"I rearranged a few interviews until CMA week," I grounded out through clenched teeth. "Needed to get back home. After talking to Sadie on my way in seems I made the right decision."

"Shit," Susanna whimpered drawing her knees up to her chest. The over-sized t-shirt she had on with leggings slipping off her shoulder. Her auburn hair pulled back in a messy low ponytail. Amber pools tinged with tears and bloodshot around the edges. "B....what did she tell you?"

"That you were drunk off your ass almost?" I snapped walking around to sit down heavily on the couch. I ran a hand over my face tugging at my beard in frustration. It was like almost having a mirror into myself ten years ago in some ways. But I was way worse. Susanna winced as she chewed the inside of her cheek hanging her head. "Or how about the part where you flashed the bartender for shots....resulting in you giving the preacher of all people an eyeful? Better yet...want to explain sending me a picture of you kissing Sadie!"

"It was funny at the time," she tried to argue batting her eyes at me. A small hand landed on my knee. "Come on. You can't sit here telling me it didn't get to you see a picture of two women kissing, both of whom you have slept with mind you. Bet it made you hard B."

"Under normal circumstances," I hissed reaching down gripping her chin in my hand hearing a gasp puff out. Yep all red wine. Sadie said it was tequila and Jack last night. "I would have been hard enough to drive nails. Luke thought it was plum fucking hilarious. Me on the other hand, it pissed me off!"

"Made you jealous did it?" Susanna asked with a hiccup arching an eyebrow at me in challenge. "I mean the two of you fucked so why are you pissed that I kissed her?"

"Because it's not you!" I yelled in frustration seeing her eyes widen in shock. "Acting like that is not my Susanna. The one who blushes when I give her a compliment. Who can dress like a reserved Sunday school teacher sometimes and still have me wondering what you have on underneath." I watched her eyes dilate with unabashed arousal at my words. I leaned closer hovering my lips over hers. "But you might wanna clean up your act Suzie Q so you can be sober enough to acknowledge when someone is rejecting you. Because let me tell you Sadie was sober as a judge that night and there was never any doubt if she was faking it or not. Screamed actually...."

A slap turned my head with the force of the hit. The sound echoing between us. A sob slipped past Susanna's trembling lips at my words. I was so far gone on being mad at her I couldn't feel the remorse for being an asshole.

"Guess it's a good fucking thing we aren't together anymore!" she screamed scrambling to her feet to get away from me. The empty glass and bottles tumbling to the floor with a crash as she backed away from me. She pointed at the door shaking. Tears streaming down her face. She went to take a step towards me but I jumped up putting my hands out not wanting her to step on the broken glass with her bare feet. Gripping her elbows, Susanna hit her fists against my chest trying to get away from me. "Just let me go and get out you asshole! I don't need you!"

"Well," I snapped seeing red. "I think that is just the alcohol talking for your stubborn ass!" A foot landed in my shin further pissing me off even if it didn't hurt. I leaned down throwing her over my shoulder. I turned the tv off as Susanna fought to get free from me. A sharp smack across her ass made her let out a frustrated ear piercing scream. I grabbed her phone off the coffee table turning towards the door with her kicking and screaming. "Fight me all you want sweetheart, but you aren't getting down."

"Just where the fuck do you think you are taking me!" Susanna yelled as I slammed the door behind me. Fists beating in my back. I tipped my hat at Mable Jenkins driving by walking to my truck. I threw Susanna in the middle stopping her tantrum with a raised finger and a glare.

"To my house," I snarled climbing in beside her with a mean smirk. "Guarandamntee not a drop of alcohol there for you to hide behind!"

Hmmm.....things seemed to be getting better but.....Make sure you zip on over to read the latest update for Crash My Party by to get the other side of how things went down and why BG is so pissed. We shall been in the teepee

Small Town Talk

S usanna's POV

"You have lost your damn mind if you think I am going in there this morning!" I hissed throwing my sunglasses onto the dash of the truck. The blinding sunlight didn't hurt as much as the glare from the man in the truck with me. Arguing had been a mild term for what we did last night. Part of me felt shame. I had been drunk this weekend. Made a fool out of myself along with him. Sadly, in this town that meant something. Part of the roles we played in the community whether we wanted to or not. Our arguments now were worse than they were when we were dating. Seeing the crowd filing into church, I let out a distressed whimper. My hair flying as I whipped my aching head back and forth. "Please B! Please don't make me go in there. They all will be staring!"

"I know," Brantley said so coldly I swore icicles where about to appear. He climbed out walking around to open my door. The rigid set to his shoulders portraying how angry he still was. I had woken up alone in his bed pulling the sheets up trying to cover up as I had started to cry. Found him downstairs in the music room laying on the couch staring at the ceiling. Had been a floor and a half between us not just another room.

Hurt more knowing that he was lying beside me when I'd succumbed to sleep then gone when I woke up.

He banded an arm around my waist yanking me out. Long fingers tangled with mine in a death grip. Rings digging into my knuckles, but I didn't dare say anything about it. There would be no fighting him to get free. The low-heeled boots I'd slipped on with my black sweater dress scraping on the concrete when I dug my heels in. A low growl made goosebumps dance over my skin and not the good kind. Seeing us walk up together eyes widened. Ever since Mama's death there was constant speculation on if we were back together. In truth, we weren't at all.

Out of the corner of my eye I saw Elmer Johnson grin holding out a hand to his poker buddies from the Moose Lodge. I knew that he had won some sort of bet. Kept my eye roll to myself as we passed. The knitting circle ceased their gossiping to blatantly stare. Brantley nodded his head giving them a charming smile. "Good morning ladies."

Granny Hale and Nana Gilbert stopped hugging us both. I saw the scrutiny in both women's eyes noticing my hangover. Like I said, small town life at it's finest. Brantley pulled me into the pew beside Mama Becky. Her eyes studied me in concern as she slid down making it where I was at least sandwiched between her and Brantley. Felt shielded from prying eyes some. At least until the preacher's wife stopped at the end of the pew. I wanted to crawl in a hole due to the death glare she shot me before asking Mama Becky a question.

B wrapped an idle arm around my shoulders brushing the hair away from my neck putting the teeth marks there on full display. The ass painted on a charming grin as the preacher's wife gasped. I wanted to die from mortification along with making a mental note to tell Steph we would need extra cinnamon rolls tomorrow. I foresaw the entire town stopping by just to catch up on the latest gossip about me. And Brantley was making it worse by how he was acting. Like a possessive asshole trying to prove a point. Wanted to kick him and stick my tongue out like I was two saying we weren't dating anymore.

"Good morning Mrs. Miller," Brantley drawled in a voice known to make fan girls toss their panties on stage. "That green really makes your eyes pop."

Sandy Miller gave him an incredulous look before turning away headed to her customary seat on the front pew. He turned back to me glancing down at my neck with a smirk. I tried to wiggle away from him only to have the iron band around my shoulders tightening making a gasp bubble out. Lips brushed my ear making me tremble. Made the raging headache I had worse. Especially when Katie Benson strolled by giving me a smirk that had me wanting to jump up putting my fist in her face. Be a way to work off some of the guilty anger I'd had simmering for months off.

"You move even an ass cheek an inch off of this pew," he warned lowly in my ear making my throat close up. "Then your sweet ass will be redder than it already is baby girl."

A throat clearing followed by the bulletin smacking the back of both of our heads broke up the narrowed eyed stare down we were engaged in. Wished I could say he had been bluffing. Heavens knows he wasn't in the slightest. Mama Becky snapped her fingers at both of us.

"Brantley Keith," she hissed laying a protective hand on my arm. I saw Stephanie and Ben settling down in the pew ahead of us with Kolby in tow. The three of them turning with rapt interest knowing something was going down. Stephanie shook her head with a sigh. "You have proved your point now stop it. You are embarrassing Susanna more than she needs."

"That's debatable," he grumbled glaring at his mama then dropping his arm from around me. I looked down at my feet hiding the tears shimmering in my eyes from everyone by the curtain of my hair. The wish that there was some kind of alcohol readily available to me would be worth millions if granted to me right now. I could hide the guilt and shame behind the liquor. A rough hand reached for mine that were curled in my lap gently lacing fingers together. I took strength from that small comfort. A low chuckle sounded making me chance a glance up. I was met with a grinning Kolby.

"So Suzie Q," he whispered leaning over the back of the pew. Stephanie raised her hand poised to hit him as Ben folded his lips to keep a laugh in. "Heard you were auditioning for the next Georgia Girl's Gone Wild."

He yelped as Stephanie grabbed his ear twisting about the time Brantley punched his shoulder. Half the congregation turned watching the show. I closed my eyes in silent prayer that either the floor would swallow me up or Jesus would appear to turn water into wine.

Brantley's POV

Closing the passenger door of my truck, I paused midway around to my side looking in the windshield. Susanna reached for her sunglasses putting them on like a shield. But I knew without seeing closely that tears were trickling down her cheeks. Some of the anger I had been clinging to since getting off the phone with Sadie abated. Worry and fear was fueling it. At times I wished I could turn it off. But the truth of it was I was worried about her. I loved her so damn much even if she thought I didn't anymore.

Which is why I struggled with how to handle all this with her. If something wasn't done she would only get worse. Little hard to give the woman you loved a swift kick in the ass even if she needed it. Turning out of the church parking lot, I reached my hand over the console laying it on her arm. Susanna sniffled before turning her head to look at me.

"You hungry?" I asked her more gently than I had since storming into her house last night. "Mama is making lunch as always. Think Steph and Ben were going by."

"I'm not," she whispered shaking her head. "I just.."

"Then let's go to the house," I said giving her a quiet smile. And here I went caving on the tough love. Maybe Sadie was right. But at the moment protective instincts were kicking in. "I'll send out a couple texts making sure nobody comes by. Let them know I'm locking the gates until tomorrow."

I saw a quick nod seeing her bottom lip tremble knowing I made the right decision for the moment. Maybe I could get her to open up to me about all that was going on instead of throwing a wall up. That was something that hurt the most out of everything. Susanna used to be able to talk to me about any and everything. But not now. No words were spoken the rest of the drive. I trailed behind Susanna going in the house sending out the few texts I needed then cut my phone on vibrate.

Walking into my room, I passed over one of my t-shirts for her as I dug out a pair of sweatpants trading my church clothes for those before heading downstairs. Quiet footsteps alerted me of her presence downstairs after I had slipped her favorite movie in the DVD player. I sat down in my recliner crooking my finger at the timid red head standing there shuffling her feet in uncertainty. Nodding my head at her favorite blanket on the couch, she picked it up stepping closer to me.

I tugged Susanna down in my lap hearing a quiet sigh. She got settled curling up against me her head resting on my shoulder. Throwing the blanket over her, I started the movie knowing it was her favorite. Let even myself get lost in the story of Noah and Allie for yet another time. I thought about the first time she begged me to watch it with her. The evil little minx got a kick out of the fact I had mentioned watching it in a couple of interviews.

Other than the soft laughs occasionally no words were spoken. Heard her sniffle a time or two on the tearjerker parts. Shifting in my arms, Susanna curled up laying across me with her head on my arm. Smoothing the silky hair away from her neck, I frowned mentally chiding myself as I stroked a finger over the marks there. While the fire had been there last night, it hadn't been for the right reasons either. Anger, hurt, worry, with just a hint of jealously had been fueling that never ending passion I had for her.

"I'm sorry," I murmured tightening my arm around her as Susanna turned her head looking at me in confusion. Then as she realized what I meant a faint blush spread across her cheeks. "I was rougher with you than I should have been."

"It's okay," she whispered sitting up to look at me. I opened my mouth to argue with her but was stopped by the pressure of her finger on my lips. "We both were pretty worked up last night in more ways than one."

"That's an understatement," I sighed leaning forward pressing my forehead to hers. "The movie is over darlin."

"I don't want to go home B," Susanna's voice wavered closing her eyes. A lone tear leaking out trailing down her cheek. "I just can't be alone in that house. Keep waiting on that phone to ring and be Mama calling with the latest gossip or to..."

"Then stay," I murmured wrapping my arms around her. Brushing my lips against hers tenderly, I pulled her closer. "Stay tonight. No one here but me and you. Whatever you need from me baby girl. I am here. Just wish you saw that."

"I do," Susanna whimpered as more tears slipped down her cheeks. "I feel so alone. It's like a part of me is missing in some ways and I can't find it."

"It's not at the bottom of a bottle baby girl," I sighed cupping her face in my hands. "You are talking to the man who used to think it was. Trust me the end result is not good. I'm terrified of losing you to it."

"Then what do I do?" she whispered brokenly. Maybe, just maybe I was getting through to her.

"Day at a time baby," I told her wiping tears away with my thumbs. "Let me take your worries and fears away even if it's just for a night. I've been here even when you are pushing me away. Let me in again even if for a little while."

Soft nod was the only answer I got as I shifted standing up with Susanna in my arms heading for the stairs. Last night had been more about anger coupled with passion for both of us. I wanted tonight to be different. It was. Lingering kisses. Soft caresses. Slowly driving her out of her mind with desire as she clung to me. Teary eyes met me as I stilled my movements feeling nails tease along my back. Locking my eyes with the amber depths mixed with longing and desire, I hovered my lips over hers.

"I love you Susanna Grace," I whispered rocking my hips forward never breaking eye contact. "Please don't ever forget that no matter what."

"I love you too," Susanna sobbed clinging to me. "So damn much."

Christmas Eve 2016 ()

Luke's POV

Bo's first Christmas is turning out to be one we won't have trouble remembering when he's older. We all gathered at Mama Becky's to have Christmas dinner, especially considering how Susanna has been coping with the loss of her mother. Sadie's parents and Mama joined also. Susanna's father politely declined according to Mama Becky and when Mama came upon this news suggested they go hogtie and bring him anyways. Thank God no one listened to her. I've already took the tequila away reminding Mama with how Susanna has been it's not the time to pass around Jose Cuervo.

The bickering between Susanna and BG wasn't bad until Susanna stumbled over a few of Bo's toys that he received from Stephanie earlier and began cussing like a sailor. BG threw her over his shoulder marching straight outside. Kolby got smacked with a wooden spoon by his mama when he grumbled over having to wait to eat. I might have received a smack in the back of the head for trying not to laugh at him also.

"It's getting worse. I knew I smelled it on her when I hugged her earlier," Sadie mumbled passing Bo over to me so she can help set the table. She disappears back into the kitchen while I sit with Ben and Stephanie. Ryleigh drags Kolby to go play but suddenly clings to him hearing BG's booming voice pierce through the wooden door.

"That's it!" Sadie stalks to the door looking like she's ready to beat someone's ass. I quickly pass Bo to Steph so I can jump in front of my ticked off girlfriend. "Move your fine ass baby because I'm about to go rip apart theirs!"

"Sadie," I try to bite back my laughter because she sure does look cute all fired up. The narrowing of her baby blues helps eliminate my laugh though. "You need to leave them be darlin. They're going to fight it out regardless if you go out there or not."

"I can hear his loudmouth yelling at her all the way in the kitchen! He scared Ryleigh!" Sadie yells then puts her hand over her screaming upon me lowering my glare. I wrap my arms around her and pull her close thanking God things aren't bad between us anymore.

"She has to work through her grief. Not saying drinking all the time is the best way but she has to find a way to handle it and hopefully she'll find something better soon. There's a lot that's gone on for her, baby. We cannot tell her how to grieve. BG losing his temper isn't helping but I get it. He doesn't want to lose her," I quietly said pushing back her brown curls she did for tonight. Sadie chews on her bottom lip glancing over at Stephanie.

We then hear BG lose his temper once more than a loud thud causing me to swing the door open. He holds up an airplane bottle of Jack with a deep growl headed at Susanna. Blood drips from his other hand and the cracks in the wooden banister tells me what took the blunt of his anger. Sadie pushes past me and immediately starts demanding what's going on as well as for BG to stop yelling so much at Susanna.

"Do you see why I'm pissed Sadie?! She was hiding this fucking bottle!" BG roared at her having me step between them pushing Sadie behind me. BG gives me a once over with dark eyes before he turns back to Susanna holding the bottle up in her face. "It's a damn good thing we don't have children together, Susanna Grace, because if I caught your ass doing this in front of them....," he trails off lowering his head in a dark, humorless chuckle. The ominous sound even has Sadie clenching tightly to my jacket watching the scene continue to unravel. BG turns from Susanna to head inside but stops in front of me hanging his head low. "I can't deal with her right now man," BG said defeatedly glancing at Sadie peering out from behind my back. He storms inside and slams the door causing both women to jump where they stood. I move towards Susanna and surprise her when I pull her in for a hug. I meet Sadie's curious blue eyes over Susanna's shoulder putting a hand up for Sadie not to come any closer.

"Go see if they need any more help darlin. Let me talk with her," I quietly said to Sadie who appears ready to argue with me but finally sighs and goes inside the house. Once she shuts the door behind her, I turn back to a glossy eyed Susanna. Tears streaming like a river down her cheeks. My heart aches for her knowing remotely close what she's feeling losing someone so close. "Susanna, I know that—,"

"You don't know Luke!" She snapped. Taking a step back, I tilt my head staring at her waiting to see if she remembers anything about me. Nope. Alcohol clouding her mind still.

"I do know okay. Lost two siblings and my brother-in-law which apparently you have forgotten. I understand you are trying to grieve darlin, but it's not healthy. It is because of you and BG that I pulled my head out of my ass realizing I couldn't lose what I love the most. I don't want to see that happen to you Susanna," I step closer wrapping an arm around her shoulders to guide her to the swing. She almost falls when she goes to sit but I steady her hearing a faint thank you choked out. She leans her head on my shoulder pushing against the porch along with me. I know she doesn't need yelling or scorning right now. She's getting that from the two of the people she loves most.

"Luke I just can't," Susanna whimpered as I put my arm around her. Her body shakes from the soft, heartbreaking sobs she doesn't hold back. "I see her everywhere when I'm awake. When I sleep, she's there but at least there she's alive and everything is okay again. The alcohol numbs the pain of losing her."

"I know the alcohol helps but do you really want to live the rest of your life using alcohol to forget she ever left? You're going down a dark path, Susie Q. Don't you remember how bad things got for me and Sadie? Hell, BG was a second away from beating my ass if I didn't straighten up," I grinned down at her feeling a little relieved to see a faint smile and chuckle come from her. "It's going to get easier but it doesn't mean that you've forgotten her. I'm not here to tell you that you need to stop grieving that's not it. Only you can decide on that. I just want you to understand darlin that there are better ways to mourn her loss than drowning yourself in the bottle. All it's doing is pushing people away which eventually you'll be mourning them also," I wipe away the last tears that have fallen down Susanna's cheeks. The telltale signs of drinking have slightly faded from her gaze. Not enough though to not give everyone reminders of what she's been doing when we walk back inside. "And don't think I don't know what you are doing either with trying to push people away, especially BG. He's not here because he feels obligated. None of us are. He loves you."

"It's so hard Luke, so damn hard. Let's not forget I spent a year gone missing holidays and special events. I just want to go back and change that," Susanna sniffled blinking away a few tears trying to come back.

"I understand why you would feel guilty but your mama wouldn't want that. She knew how much that was your dream. She also wouldn't want you handling her death this way. We are going to get through this," I said with a light laugh seeing Susanna whip her head around scrunching up her face. "Yes darlin I said we. All of us," I smiled at her getting a smile as well from her. I note the time on my watch knowing they are about ready to serve dinner. If we aren't in there soon then I know my girlfriend will be coming out here dragging us inside. "Just remember that grief is a lot like the ocean. Times of rough, treacherous waves but also periods of calm and steady. You just have to learn how to swim, Susie Q." I stand up offering her my hand. Pulling her into a hug, she holds tight quietly sniffling into my chest. She pulls away letting out a deep breath running a hand through her hair. Smoothing out her clothes, she gives me a small smile.

"Guess we should go back in there huh?" Susanna said with a light laugh. Nodding, I loop my arm through hers heading towards the door.

"If you want to sit between me and Ryleigh then go right on ahead darlin. I know with things between you and BG it might be hard to sit beside him. He would love for you too even if he's pissed. But I also know that you might not feel up to and it's okay not to," I mumbled just in case someone is being nosey on the other side of this door. I can count at least three women inside right now who would be. Susanna agreed with a nod and I open the door for her.

Everyone goes silent upon us walking inside. Mama Becky breaks the awkward silence by saying let's say grace. Susanna walks around to the empty chair on my right. When I pull it out for her, I can feel the angry stare from BG directed at the both of us. His eyes meet mine then sighs. Once we say grace, BG looks over at Susanna with hurt and anger but locks it down before she notices. He joins in the story Kolby is telling about some girl and acts as if Susanna isn't here anymore.

"How is she?" Sadie whispered into my ear from my left. Leaning over putting my arm around the back of her chair, I lean in close but before I can speak I catch a short glance from BG.

"She's at least here baby. For now that's all that matters," I kiss her cheek before leaning away. Sadie's hand rests on my leg reminding me that if Sadie and I can pull out from the dark place we were at then Susanna and BG can also. They have to.

Thank you to my evil partner for Luke's POV. Yes...I know....I'm in the teepee for this.... Hopefully things will get better soon. Well maybe...

Wake Up Call

J anuary 2017

Susanna's POV

I took an idle sip from the glass of wine in my hand lost in my thoughts. I rested my chin on my raised knees staring into the fire I had started once the sun had gone down. I swear it was like I couldn't get warm. Stephanie was still pissed at me for the other day at the bakery. I swore if she told me one more time I had a problem I was going to flip my shit. The holidays had been tougher than I imagined. I'd handled them how I thought I needed to. Luke had been the only one who had made sense.

I winced thinking about the huge argument between Brantley and I on Christmas Eve which was horrible. I was out of the sleeping pills I got months ago and refused to get anymore. Red wine did the job most days. That or the rare night I slept in Brantley's arms. Well depended on who was checking on me that particular day. Like didn't they realize it was predictable now. The never ending guilt was eating me alive. I turned the glass up finishing it off feeling the warmth spreading through my veins getting lost watching the dancing flames.

So lost in thought I didn't hear the door open or close never realizing I wasn't alone until the couch dipped. Knew it was someone with a key because I'd locked up when I got home from the bakery. An arm wrapped around my neck pulling me back into a warm chest. Shiver going down my spine when lips brushed my ear. Cool nose brush against my cheek. Guess it had gotten colder outside after dark.

"What you in such deep thought about Suzie Q?" Brantley murmured pressing a kiss to my cheek. He laid his chin on my shoulder as I turned my head looking at him. Green eyes narrowed at the empty glass in my hand. I sighed leaning over to sit it on the table by the couch before leaning back. An absent sigh slipped past his lips. Here we go again. "I'm tired of having this argument with you darlin. So damn tired of having it."

"Then stop bringing it up," I snapped feeling my gut churn at the haunted look in his eyes. I put that there. Me. The woman who claimed to love him. I lifted my hands covering my face. "I can't do this tonight B. Just one time. Swear it's all we do anymore. I can't tell you the last time I got an actual smile from you. Don't even know why you keep coming by. You have no reason to."

"You know why," he snarled gruffly. He closed his eyes with a tired sigh leaning against the back of the couch slumping down kicking his boots up on the coffee table. A wry chuckle slipped out making me raise an eyebrow at him. "Guess I'm gonna be wrong in hoping there is one of those death by chocolate cakes you make sitting in the kitchen?"

"Huh?" I asked distractedly blinking away the slight buzz I had going. Guess I should have chosen the hidden bottle of Jack stuck in a big bag of sugar I kept in the pantry. Only Stephanie might be the one who discovered that one. A defeated sigh sounded from the man beside me as he closed his eyes. Other than his sweet tooth I was trying to think of why I'd have his favorite cake on hand. Then it hit me. I covered my face with a groan feeling tears well in my eyes. "Shit B. I am so, so sorry."

"It's fine Suzie Q," he muttered smothering a yawn. He had been on the road doing radio tour for the new album coming out next week. An album even though there was an advanced copy laying on my desk in the den, I was still hesitant to listen to. Man wrote about what he knew so made me afraid in some ways. "Just another day..."

I stopped him with a finger on his lips. Keeping my eyes locked on his, I crawled into his lap seeing his eyes widened. Been a while since I had made the first move. I pressed my lips to his taking him by surprise kissing him deeply. Felt a slight grimace against my lips knowing he tasted the red wine I had been drinking. Knew he wasn't happy with me over it. But I couldn't take it back at the moment. Big hands gripped my hips teasing the edges of my sweatshirt while I deepened the kiss just wanting to feel something other than sadness or anger for a little while. I broke the kiss with a gasp laying my forehead against Brantley's raising my hands to cup his face.

"Happy Birthday B," I whispered kissing him softly. "I'm sorry I forgot. I got busy with the bakery and you've been gone. If you want I think I have the stuff for that cake here at the house. Icing left over from the bakery."

"Or," he chuckled darkly sliding a hand up tangling his fingers in the loose strands of my hair tugging slowly. "We can skip the cake just going for the icing. You can be my birthday cake."

"Well then," I giggled with a flirty laugh reaching for the buttons of the red and black flannel he was wearing getting a teasing smirk in return. I got it undone enough to find what I was looking for leaning down to swirl my tongue over the letters on his chest savoring the feel of warm skin under my lips. A taste that was all him had me rocking my hips against him.

A growl sounded before I was flipped over on my back making me giggle. Lips landing on mine while I wove my arms around his neck tugging the black beanie he had on off. Teeth nipped my bottom lip making me arch my chest into the wandering hands moaning lowly in the back of my throat. A buzzing came from Brantley's pocket vibrating against my raised leg.

"Dammit," he huffed with a growl shifting to yank it out. He showed me it was Luke calling and hit ignore tossing his phone on the coffee table leaning down to capture my lips hard. I was working his shirt over his head when my phone sounded from the coffee table. I froze recognizing Luke's ringtone. Brantley felt me freeze breaking the kiss looking down at me. "What? He will leave a message baby girl."

"B," I said feeling icy fear wash over me as I reached for the phone. Worry churning my stomach. I shifted reaching for my phone answering it. I knew if he called Brantley like that then followed up with me something was wrong with either the kids or Sadie. "Hello."

"Sadie had a wreck!" Luke roared in my ear making me gasp. Brantley's eyes met mine as he sat up pulling me with him. "I don't know if her and the kids are okay! I haven't even seen her yet. Y'all..."

"On our way," I answered as Brantley pulled me to my feet pushing me towards my room. Heard him murmur pack a bag in my ear not covered by the phone. Luke hung up as I fluttered around grabbing stuff I thought I would need throwing them in a bag. Brantley paced running a worried hand over his face as tears welled in my eyes. I covered my mouth to keep a sob in. He stepped closer wrapping his arms around me hugging me tight as I clung to him. "She's got to be okay. Those babies have got to be okay. It will....."

"Baby," Brantley murmured tipping my chin up shaking his head. "Don't think like that okay. Grab your charger and let's go. I have a bag in my truck. Come on."

Ten minutes later he had his truck on the interstate headed north to Nashville. I sat in the passenger seat wringing my hands in worry. The yellow and white lines blurred as tears slipped down my cheeks. I don't know what I would do if something happened to Sadie. We were finally getting our friendship back on track some. I just finished the design for Bo's birthday cake the other day. Brantley's eyes were focused on the road as he weaved in and out of traffic like he was driving in the Daytona 500.

A few hours into the drive Luke updated me with a text that she was out of surgery. I breathed a slight sigh of relief. Hearing the familiar opening bars to a haunting song, I reached across the console grabbing Brantley's hand as he heard it too. "Drink A Beer" sounded through the truck with only my sniffles and the noises from the highway accompanying it. We spent the rest of the drive in silence both of us willing the miles to pass faster.

Finally reaching the hospital, we stepped off the floor. I froze as the elevator closed after us. Brantley took a step then realized I wasn't behind him. All I could think about was is this how Daddy felt getting to the hospital that night? Brantley turned back holding a big hand out for mine lacing our fingers together. He squeezed gently then guided me behind him down the hall. We found the room easing the door open. Luke had his head down clasping Sadie's hand that wasn't in a cast.

Ryleigh and Bo were curled up in the other chair together sleeping. I noted the few scrapes and bruises on each of the kids glad they seemed to be unscathed otherwise. Luke jerked his head up blinking his red rimmed eyes seeing us. He kissed Sadie's hand before standing to hug us both. Our quiet conversation made Ryleigh to stir. A grin teased her lips seeing us as she moved waking Bo up who let out a disgruntled whine.

"Uncle B. Miss Suzie," Ryleigh whispered after Luke reminded her to be quiet. He stepped around scooping Bo up as Ryleigh tackled us. Brantley scooped up as she flung her arms around both of our necks. I pressed a kiss to her cheek. B let out a quiet chuckle hearing a disgruntled growl coming from Luke's arms. Bo was pissed about being left out. Ryleigh wiggled down as Luke passed a grouchy Bo over to Brantley who threw his arms around his neck clinging tight. A bittersweet tug at my heart at the sight of them. Bo turned his head with a grin looking at me.

"Ookie?" he asked sweetly batting his eyes making me smile. I leaned over kissing his cheek as Brantley and Luke chuckled.

"I don't have any with me this time buddy," I told him gently. "I'm sorry." Ryleigh leaned into my side as Brantley sat down with Bo in his lap trying to wrestle with him. I kissed the top of her head wrapping her in a hug. "Glad you two are okay. Mama will be okay as well."

"They got lucky considering it was a drunk driver," Luke murmured lowly. My gut felt like lead as he spoke the words. Knew another set of eyes were watching me carefully. "Sadie should wake up soon. Glad they are all relatively okay."

"I know she will," Ryleigh said with a quiet smile on her face. Her arms tightened around me. "Mrs. Connie told me she would be. She tried her best to make sure Bo and I and Mama were all okay. But she knew Mama would choose us to be okay first. Held both of our hands tight. Helped me from being so scared until the ambulance arrived. Reassured us Daddy would get to us soon." I gasped letting out a whimper at her words. I looked up meeting Luke's teary eyes as Brantley shifted Bo in his arms watching me carefully. "As they got there she kissed both our cheeks telling me she would keep an eye on Mama now."

Not long after Sadie woke up groggy and happy to see the kids unscathed. A little more time passed as she reminded Brantley and I both she was okay.

Apologizing for the scare on his birthday of all days even though we were into the early hours of the next day now. He growled at her rolling his eyes muttering like that mattered. A smack from me to his arm shushed him knowing Sadie would have done the same if she hadn't been laying in a hospital bed. Ryleigh tugged my arm telling me she was hungry.

Bo was asleep with his head on B's shoulder. Sadie shared a look with Luke suggesting they take the kids to get something to eat. That Brantley would need some coffee before we got back on the road. He had grumbled starting to argue but then remembered I had mentioned the radio tour to her on the phone. He was due to leave back out tomorrow for another before tour rehearsals. I volunteered to stay with her. After they headed out I pulled the chair closer reaching for her hand. Damn had I missed her.

"Sadie," I mumbled squeezing her good hand only to be stopped with a slow shake of her head.

"Don't apologize to me Suzie Q," she sighed closing her eyes. Blue orbs with a shimmer of tears faced me when they reopened. "It's all water under the bridge. Everything and I do mean everything. I'll be fine. We all know Luke is going to pamper me until I'm ready to kill him. I just want you to be okay honey."

"I'm trying," I sniffled looking down at the white sheets on the bed. Wiping at my eyes with my free hand. "I really am trying."

"Good," Sadie murmured. "Because I need my best friend. And that damn outlaw loves you more than life itself. Don't forget it."

By mid-morning we were headed back to Georgia. Luke swore to me he would keep me posted on everything. Sadie had threatened to ear tug us both if we didn't get back home. I flipped the console up stretching out putting my head in Brantley's lap as he droved down the interstate. A big hand laced with mine resting on my chest as I dozed off. Had tried to get him to let me drive but he had refused me. I drifted off to sleep listening the hum of the tires on the highway.

I walked into the kitchen following the humming seeing Mama with her back to me. I hurried closer throwing my arms around her neck making her jump.

"Susanna Grace," she admonished with a chuckle. "You scared me child. What are you doing?"

"Hugging you," I sighed feeling her turn pulling me into her arms. Felt more comforted than I had in a long time. "I've missed you."

"Miss you too sweetie," Mama murmured squeezing me back. She pulled away cupping my cheeks in her soft hands. Pursed lips greeted me. "Now I ask again, what are you doing? Drinking is not like you daughter of mine. Not like this."

"It's so hard Mama," I sobbed as she pushed me down onto a barstool leaning on the island looking down at me as tears flowed. A sharp smack to the back of my head made me yelp. "Mama!"

"You needed that honey!" she growled putting her hands on her hips. "Grieving me is not in a bottle. God knows your Daddy hasn't been much help bless his heart. Praise Jesus Brantley, Sadie, and Steph have been on your ass."

"I feel so guilty!" I yelled feeling it all bubbling to the surface. Mama's eyes glittered with tears listening to me. "I missed my last Christmas with you because I was being selfish! I broke the heart of the man I love more than anything because I thought I just had to further my career. Which was doing just fine without all of that. I'm hurting him further by drinking like I have been. I let down my best friends and my family in so many ways. I've let so many people down Mama. I don't deserve how good they have been to me. How much longer will B put up with this?"

"Then do better!" Mama snapped shaking her finger at me.

"I also feel so guilty about the fight we had the night before your wreck," I sobbed brokenly. I remembered her fussing at me for being mad at Sadie even though she understood why. Reminded me that Brantley wouldn't wait around forever for me to pull my head out of my ass. It hadn't been pretty.

"Baby," she whispered pressing a kiss to the top of my lowered head. "I forgave you as soon as I was done. Be the woman I raised you to be honey. I love you daughter of mine. Let that man love you through everything just like he has. If you do that everything will work out."

I jerked awake with a gasp sitting up so fast Brantley almost ran off the road. Clutching my chest, I turned meeting his wide eyes.

"Susanna," he said narrowing his eyes as tears streamed down my face. I sobbed shaking my head feeling my chest grow tight with each deep cry. Felt the truck ease of to the side of the interstate as he threw it into park. Warm arms wrapped around me hugging me tight. Knew his mind was racing with what could be wrong with me. I clung to him as finally my sobs quieted down. Taking a deep breath, I pulled back meeting his worried eyes.

"I need you to call Dr. Collins B," I whispered seeing confusion in his eyes at my words.

"Okay," he answered reaching for his phone on the dash. "Baby girl you sick?"

"No," I said lowly. I puffed out a shaky breath laying my hands on his chest as understanding washed over his face. "I need help B. It's time I got some."

She's making a step she needs to. Took her being the one to accept it. Not everyone telling her. To see how she is doing with it all stay tuned for to drop the next update for Crash My Party sooon....

Hopefully I can come out of the teepee soon.

What We Think We Want

M^{ay 2017}

Susanna's POV

I groggily felt myself coming up from the dredges of the exhausted sleep I had slipped into during the early hours of the morning. The last few months had been life changing and a learning process in many ways. I'd started it out on my own in a few ways because it had to be up to me to get better not anyone else. Then when sleep was eluding me and Stephanie was swearing I was trying out to be an extra for The Walking Dead, I'd shamefully tried to slip into old habits.

The end result had been me parked firmly on a tour bus the days of the week Brantley wasn't in town. Stephanie had ear tugged me off my couch and onto the gleaming black bus parked in the middle of the street making Ben almost roll with laughter. PJ was kind enough to film it for prosperity meaning it was sent to Sadie and Luke after he quit laughing. Daddy and I both had been doing grief counseling. It was helping. Had to remind myself things like this took time and I had all the support I needed.

Pushing the comforter away from my face, I stuck my arm out yawning and reaching for my phone. I noticed the new emails awaiting me. One from one of our suppliers caused my eyes to roll. But one had a gasp bubble out as I jerked clicking on it. What in the world could this be about? The iron grip around my waist shifted as a rough groan sounded near my ear. Long leg shifted being thrown over my hip pinning me deeper into the bed.

"Baby girl," Brantley murmured drowsily in my ear. That rough morning voice making me shiver. Don't think I would ever get tired of hearing it. "Why are you even awake? This is the first morning in two weeks there hasn't been anyone pounding on the side of the bus eagerly trying to find out what you made for breakfast. The only thing keeping Ben from scaling the fence since we are home is that he has missed Steph. PJ was bitching the other day that his jeans are getting tight."

"I know," I chuckled even though my mind was racing at the words written in that email. Fear was flowing through my veins. There was no easy answer to the question asked in it. I looked over my shoulder at the relaxed face knowing if I hushed he would drift back to sleep. "He was grumbling the other night. Asked him if I needed to make healthy pancakes for him. Would hate for a fan girl to get past him mauling you."

"More like have to lock you on the bus again," he drawled pressing a kiss to the back of my neck as I tensed up. I really shouldn't have had the reaction I did that night. Wasn't my place in some ways. I mean technically we weren't together. But we'd quickly fallen into old habits the last few months. "Walked off stage that night to him snickering saying "Boss, Cupcake was madder than hell at ol girl flashing those double D's at you."

"I shouldn't have been like that," I sighed my phone weighing a million pounds in my hand. Closing my eyes, I willed the unsure tears away. "Don't have any...."

"If you say you don't have any right to feel that way Susanna Grace," Brantley growled lowly in my ear pulling me closer than I already was. "I'm going to smack your ass. Is it you laying in my arms right now? Yes, mam it is. There is no one else I want here. Haven't wanted anyone else here. Has the last two years been a roller coaster pain in the ass? Yes they have, but baby, still hasn't changed how I feel about you."

"Before you finish your little speech," I sighed sitting up. I looked down at him passing my phone over. "You need to read that."

Brantley studied me for a minute then took the phone from my out-stretched hand. Saw his sleepy eyes read over the email I'd received. His lips flattened into a thin line raising an eyebrow.

"Ma petite my ass," he growled still reading. "Can I put a bullet in his frenchiefied ass for even using that name for you? Think he needs a good ass kicking to remind him not to tread on another man's woman." I gasped at his words even though I knew he meant them. What surprised me was when he sat up nonchalantly handing me my phone back. A slow kiss pressed to my lips before rolling away to climb out of bed. His black UGA shorts dipping on his hips as he stretched making. I was too surprised at his response to appreciate the ripple of muscles and ink. Brantley looked over his shoulder at my dropped jaw. "Wanting you to help launch the bakery chain he is planning in Europe. It's an amazing opportunity baby."

He turned heading into his closet like it was just another day. Like I hadn't just dropped the bomb of me potentially going back to France in his lap. Heard what sounded like the code for the gun safe in there being entered. What in the hell was he doing? Gonna actually grab a gun and go shoot Jacques? I groaned dropping my phone covering my face with my hands like this is B I am talking about. That was a high possibility. Tears burned my eyes. Could I do this? Look at what happened with my life when I left the first time. What I would be giving up by going. The starting salary alone was enough to pour back into my business here to expand if Stephanie was up for it.

The bed dipped as my hands were pulled away from my face. My face was cupped tenderly before lips brushed against mine and something soft was pressed into my hand. Brantley lifted his head kissing my forehead before standing up. I looked down at the square black velvet box feeling my eyes grow huge. He walked towards the bathroom. "That is yours to do with what you want baby girl. Sell it and use for the bakery or as a paper weight for your desk in France. It is up to you. However, there is always another option. But I can't make the decision for you."

When I heard the shower turn on, I cracked open the box risking taking a peak. I dropped it like a hot potato at the blinding diamond ring cover my mouth in shock. Oh my God, was that really what I thought it was?

Sadie's POV ( )

A million thoughts race through my mind pulling into the airport parking garage. A late night phone call from Susanna last night asking if I would be home for the next few days has prompted this drive to Nashville International Airport. She needed a break from Georgia she claimed. I was excited because I haven't seen her since Ryleigh's birthday party but then my excitement was suddenly tampered down when she said do not tell B. Before I could question her, she quickly spit out she would send me an email with her flight information. I wanted to call back and demand she tell me why she is asking suspicious but then if I did, she may not come.

Susanna stands near baggage claim with her head down and a familiar black hat covering her hair. Black shades concealing her appearance also. Intere sting... she's definitely not wanting anyone to recognize her. There's been photos of her and Brantley popping up when he's in town but nothing too outrageous. The looming question of are they or aren't they seems to occupy the photos' headlines. I haven't told Brantley either that she had planned a visit. Threatened Luke with no sex until Christmas if he uttered a word to him. His lips are sealed.

We smiled at one another once Susanna sees me approaching the baggage claim. She hugs me as if it has been longer than a couple months since we've last seen one another. Not much is said during our walk to Luke's truck or even during the ride to the house. Susanna keeps her gaze steady outside the window having me become more worried about why she is here. I last spoke to Brantley a few days ago and nothing seemed any different than it has been between the two for the last year. Something pushed this impromptu visit from my favorite baker.

Luke welcomes Susanna into a big hug the moment she steps inside the house. Ryleigh steals her for a hug next before Til and Bo get one of their own. Luke takes her overnight bag while I drag Susanna into the kitchen. She chews on her bottom lip pacing back and forth in front of the kitchen while I fix a pot of coffee. Bo waddles into the kitchen squealing with Luke chasing behind him. Susanna watches them unlike I've ever seen before. There's a want behind those amber-colored eyes. There's a Mama Susie peeking through the window of her soul watching Luke toss our giggling little one in the air. She catches me smiling at her suddenly becoming her sweet blushing self. She grabs the creamer out the fridge and quickly walks to the table avoiding my watchful gaze. Luke kisses me on the cheek on the way out the kitchen taking Bo with him.

"Alright Susanna start talking. I'm glad to see you but something sent you my direction and not just to take a break from Georgia," I said placing a mug of coffee in front of her before sitting beside her. She takes off the black hat she's been wearing staring at it with a longing look. Biting her bottom lip, she reaches into her purse. Susanna places a black box on the table with a heavy sigh. She snaps her eyes upward at me when I let out a humorless chuckle.

"Well I'll be," I drawled out sliding the ring box over. I opened it up and turn it upside down shaking it. "I've been wondering if he would ever shake the dust off this thing." I grinned at Susanna who appears surprised that I'm not shocked to see a big ass rock.

"What do you mean dust? You knew?" Susanna asked shockingly. I can feel the evil twinkle in my eye wink at her while I smirk. "How long has he been planning this?"

"Honey he's been planning this since before you left for France. Had the ring burning a hole in his pocket that day," I told her pushing the ring box back across the table. Her mouth slightly gapes staring at the ring differently than she did when she first took the box out. It's as if the importance of the ring suddenly went beyond an indescribable value. "This is why you came huh?"

"Yeah," she said breathlessly. "I received another offer to go back to France. When I told him, he handed it over. That I can do what I want with it," she places the opened box back on the table. She drops her head into her hands letting out a frustrated sigh. "Why would be do that Sadie? Just here you go! He didn't even try to caveman me into marrying me!"

"Well what do you expect after everything that has happened between y'all? He's not going to stop you from going to France if you have another opportunity Susanna. That's why he didn't ask you that day you told him about the letter because he wasn't going to take away your dream just so he could have his with you," I reached over resting a hand over hers. A tear rolls down her cheek as we share a quiet glance until Bo comes toddling into the kitchen. He comes straight to me lifting his arms up to be picked up.

"Pwetty Mama," Bo said reaching for the ring once he sits in my lap. I push it away and he decides to slide back down from my lap seeing Luke come into the kitchen. Susanna watches him with a soft smile being picked up by his daddy. Luke lets out a low whistle checking out the diamond ring that needs to be on Susanna's left hand.

"That's a nice rock darlin," Luke winked with his signature smirk. Bo leans down trying to grab it again but Luke moves away before Bo can swipe it. "No bud that's not yours but it would be nice though to get Mama one of her own don't ya think?" Luke grinned moving even further away upon seeing my narrowed eyes.

"Anyways," I rolled my eyes taking a sip of my coffee so I can hide behind the mug for a bit. "So what are you going to do? France or B?"

"I don't know. France would be a great opportunity to take again. Then there's Brantley. I would love to marry him but...," Susanna glances over to Bo holding onto Luke while he takes something out the cabinet. The corner of her lip turns up but she flattens her lips into a straight line looking back at me. "...I don't see how he can still love me after all I've put him through."

Luke chimed in, "Well when you are in love with the right person you just cannot fully walk away because they are always on your mind." He walked around the kitchen island putting Bo on his feet. Crossing his arms over his chest, he continued trying to help Susanna see the truth, "It hasn't been easy but BG never stopped loving you. Never gave up on you either even if it seemed like he had at times. Sometimes we have to act like you crazy women don't phase us." He laughed walking over pressing a kiss on top of her head. He leaves out the kitchen while Ryleigh and Til run pass him both laughing til they reach the side door to go outside.

"Don't you want this Susie Q? Little outlaws running around while you dance along in the kitchen whipping up amazing recipes?" I smiled over at my friend who stares in the direction where Til and Ryleigh went.

"I don't want to be alone doing it, you know raising a family and all," Susanna mumbled glancing away while sipping her coffee. I roll my eyes that she catches when looking back at me. "What?"

"You must be out of your damn mind," I laughed shaking my head. "I guess Mama Becky is chopped liver then because there's no way she would help out," I said sarcastically. This woman is crazy if she thinks Brantley's mama would not help out. She is waiting on the edge of her seat for grandbabies. "Hell, I'll loan you LeClaire," I snorted picking up my coffee cup. I guess it's understandable why she would feel this way considering how things have been for her.

"You're right. Mama Becky would help. Steph too," Susanna nodded thoughtfully.

"Exactly. I understand you afraid of being alone, but you are never alone because you have us. Mama Becky, LeClaire, Steph, Tiff....hell even Sir Assshaker has been there for you. But the ultimate person that will be there for you as much as he can be will be Brantley. Even when he's not physically there he will be emotionally as much as people find that hard to believe," I snickered with Susanna doing the same. "This last year has sucked. No one ever really left you. You will always have a family to support you."

"I guess I have some thinking to do," she said with a light laugh. She takes the ring box closing it and puts it away in her purse. Her sudden poker face has me wondering what her decision will be. I pray she chooses the one that will give her the most happiness. Lord knows B will never stop making her happy for the rest of their days.

Thank you to my evil counterpart for Sadie's insight. Had it longer than you thought huh Suzie Q...... wonder what her answer will be??

Do As You Wish

S usanna's POV

I stuck my hand in the window paying the taxi driver before turning to take a deep breath of the humid Louisiana air that clung to me as soon as I landed. Damn, just thought it had been muggy in Georgia. Shifted my bag and purse on my shoulder letting out a deep breath stepping to one of the two buses idling on the narrow street beside the House of Blues in New Orleans.

I'd smiled at the irony when I pulled up Brantley's schedule before Luke took me to the airport earlier. Then I remembered the pop up show being added a few weeks ago. I typed in the code for the bus stepping on finding it empty. Must still be doing soundcheck. I walked to the back sitting my bag down. I eased the box into the pocket of my hunter green sundress before wringing my hands.

I had an answer but wasn't so sure it was the one he wanted to hear. Doubt circled through my veins. The door opening again and laughing voices outside made my heart race. I walked out of the back bedroom stopping halfway past the bunks chewing on my bottom lip. Brantley didn't see me since he was intent on typing something on his phone. My phone chimed in my hand making him jerk his head up with wide eyes. A sigh of relief sounded out as he stalked towards me.

"Dammit Susanna," he grumbled scooping me up in his arms. "I was worried. Stephanie said you weren't at home. Sadie swore she hadn't seen you. Don't scare me like that again."

"I just needed to get out of Georgia and think," I admitted biting my lip seeing eyes narrow down at me. "I'm sorry I scared you B. I really am. Here I am though. Not a scratch on me."

"Tempted to warm that ass," he grumped leaning down to kiss me softly. A giggle slipped out making him pull back. An eyebrow arched at me. "What?"

"Then if you get me you will have to get Sadie too," I snickered. "She lied because I asked her to. Threatened Luke with his life to stay quiet too. I went to Nashville. I needed to talk to my best friend."

"Wait til I see her again," Brantley sighed as I looked down at my sandal covered feet. Finger under my chin pulled my eyes up to meet his. I could see him searching for an answer on why I disappeared on him even if it was for a day. And after he had left to head out on the road. "Baby....."

"Think we can take a walk?" I asked shifting my feet nervously. I got a quick smile as he nodded holding a hand out for mine. Dark shades slipped back over his eyes as we walked off the bus. Brantley stopped letting PJ know we were taking a walk that he would be back. I fell in step beside him enjoying the weight of his hand in mine. Wondered how much longer I would get to enjoy the feeling. After a couple of blocks, I chanced a look at him. The cut off t-shirt, a pair of jeans Mama Becky and I both had threatened to toss out because of the holes in them, and that black hat backwards. A couple people had done double takes but no one had stopped us.

We reached Jackson Square after a little while. Laughing as we people watched. One squealing fan girl had stopped him for an autograph a couple streets back. Sitting down on one of the shaded benches, I remembered Brantley teasing me about falling in love with the roses the time he brought me down here. We'd had so much fun that trip just enjoying being together. I remember at the time I'd tried to not let the fact there was no said title for us bother me. Now, after all that we'd been through it seemed trivial. I laid my head on his shoulder feeling his arm pull me close. Wished I could stay like this forever.

"What is it Susanna?" he asked lowly. I lifted my head looking up at him. Eyes covered by shades, but I could sense the questions there. Wondering if I was going again. It really was an amazing opportunity. But was it worth the cost? Lose all the progress I'd made the last few months. Learned I didn't really have a problem with alcohol, had a problem with using it to cope with my grief. The man sitting beside me had patiently been there every step of the way even when I wanted to push him away. All because he loved me. Brantley huffed out a sigh slumping down on the bench easing his arm from around me. "So tell me, was Jacques cutting back flips over the fact you said yes. I mean he is lucky to have you doing this. You're gonna rock at it Suzie Q. Worth more than he is offering you to start actually."

"B," I said laying a hand on his arm. But didn't stop his rambling.

"And you love Paris in the fall," Brantley muttered leaning forward resting his elbows on his knees. One bouncing up and down. "That café you swear has the best hot chocolate in the world. And..."

"Brantley Keith," I said snapping my fingers. I lifted my hand covering his mouth glaring. "Would you hush for two seconds. Please?" He nodded slowly. A smile tugged at my lips as I slid my hand up pulling his shades off sitting them to the other side of me. The unsure look in his eyes haunting me. He was trying so hard to be supportive. Fairly sure locking me on that bus permanently is really what he wanted to do. "B. I'm not going. I told him I wasn't taking the job."

"Really?" he asked sounding so hopeful I knew the right decision had been made. "But it was..."

"This," I waved my hand around with a quiet laugh trying to encompass the French Quarter that we were in the heart of. "Is the closest thing to French I want to be around unless I am cooking B. My life is in Georgia. My home. My business. My family. My heart. All rooted in that red Georgia clay. So, with that said." I bit my lip slipping my hand into my pocket pulling out the ring box reaching for his hand laying it in his palm. A tear trailed down my cheek as his face fell. He clenched his fist until I opened my mouth. "Why don't you try actually asking me like Mama Becky would expect you to? Since according to Sadie you have been holding onto this for a little while. Which I am gonna ask, how long B?"

"Well," he chuckled shaking his head. Long fingers flipped the lid of the box open making my heart race. Especially at the content grin on his face as he winked at me. He lifted the glittering diamond out the sunlight seeming to make it glow. Brantley sucked in a deep breath meeting my eyes. "I had planned to ask you when you flew to Dallas to tell me about first offer to go to Paris. I wasn't going ask once you told me because I was afraid you'd turn it down and miss the opportunity. Then I was going to ask Christmas that year. And as we both know, well, things went to hell after that. Your Daddy will finally be able to let out a sigh of relief. Asked me last week after church if I was ever gonna man up." I gasped then shook my head. Sounded just like that man.

Brantley slid off the bench lowering to his knee in front of me reaching for my hand. Felt his tremble holding mine as the damn on the tears I was holding back broke. He nervously licked his lips. Green orbs locked with mine with so much love shining there I never wanted to stop seeing it.

"Susanna Grace Hale, I love you with everything in me. You love the man I once was, the one I struggle to be every day, and the man I want to be. I want forever with you. You have my heart baby girl. Have had it for a long, long time. The one. The reason God made me. I will forever be grateful if you will be my wife. So please, please put this nervous man out of his misery baby girl."

"Yes," I chuckled wiping at my eyes with my free hand. Felt my whole world click right into place as Brantley slid that gorgeous ring on my finger. I let out a yelp as he jumped to his feet lifting me up spinning me around in a circle. A booming laugh coming from him made people around us stop and stare. Carefully he lowered me to my feet leaning down to capture my lips in a deep kiss. A cheer from a group passing had him breaking the kiss with a chuckle. I stood on my tip toes wrapping my arms around him kissing him again. "I love you."

"Love you too baby girl," he chuckled wrapping an arm around me tugging me away from the growing crowd. Pretty sure I heard someone scream "That's Brantley Gilbert!" He looked over his shoulder increasing his pace towards the line of horse drawn carriages ahead of us. "Shit. We got to go."

Five furious minutes later, a carriage was winding its way through the narrow street of the French Quarter back to the buss. The driver had laughed once Brantley explained the urgency along with paying him double. I looked down at our laced hands at the ring on my finger. I tamped down the guilt knowing it should have already been on my finger. Reminded myself that everything had a rhyme and reason. Settling my head further onto his shoulder I sighed in contentment pretty sure Mama was ecstatic as she watched over us. No doubt in my mind of that.

Well now....she said yes. Stay tuned for maybe a sneaky peek at the wedding coming from in Crash My Party.

This Is Where I Belong

O ctober 2017

Susanna's POV

Bouncing down the stairs, I was slightly shocked at how quiet the house was. My canine counterpart making every step I did. Right as my foot touched the bottom step I felt my world spin being tipped backwards. I let out a yelp that was only silenced as a pair of lips landed on mine. Laughing green eyes locked with mine when the kiss ended. The content happiness in them assured me that I was right where I needed to be. Not one ounce of regret on passing over the job some people would consider the offer of a lifetime. Those people didn't have the man holding them like they were the most precious thing in the world. Sylo darted between our legs letting out a quiet bark up at Brantley who rolled his eyes. He reached down ruffling the top of his head keeping his arms firmly around me. Since officially moving in we both knew he listened to me better than B.

"Have to share her buddy," he snickered tucking a loose strand of auburn hair behind my ear with a wink. "She was mine first."

"You aren't supposed to be here," I admonished him playfully. I tugged the end of his beard pulling his lips to mine again. "Your mama explicitly said so. I was to have the house to myself today. I fibbed to her saying you stayed on the bus last night when she texted me ten minutes ago. She's picking me up in twenty minutes to go to Athens for the day. Can't let anyone around here know what we are up to." I grimaced a little as he chuckled. "Heaven help me since you are sending me with her and LeClaire both."

"Well baby girl," Brantley laughed. "Someone has two keep those two out of the tequila."

"Think they will all show?" I asked biting my lip. Brantley scoffed shaking his head prompting me to hit his leather covered chest. "It's a legit question babe. We did spring this on everyone. Though I don't know who got more excited Daddy or LeClaire. Did you know they have included him on their margarita nights? She and Mrs. Dawn signed him up for Tinder last week. Apparently the high school football coach is a hot ticket item."

"He was grumbling about all the casseroles that have been dropped off," he said making me roll my eyes. Didn't these cougars know how to be subtle. It was actually quite hilarious in some ways. Or it was until Marley, Ruby Johnson's niece who was fresh off divorce number three moved back to town. Eyed my daddy like a piece of steak last week walking into church. Was actually laughable to see her push those fake boobs courtesy of husband number two up a little higher until those batting blue eyes raked over my fiancée as well. "Like they don't already know between you, Mama, and Mrs. Dawn he's well fed. Lord your mama would have found this hilarious."

"I know she would have," I laughed softly. Heard my phone chime in the pocket of the hoodie I was wearing. I pulled it out grinning as I read the text from Sadie demanding to know what was going on. One from Mama Becky chimed next that she was ten minutes out. Sliding it back into my pocket, I stood on my tiptoes pressing my lips to his with a smile before pushing Brantley away. "You better get out of here mister before your mama gets here. You weren't supposed to come back to the house until after we left. Wondering what is going on is already the talk of town. Stephanie said half the Moose Lodge a.k.a The Liars Club came in this morning wanting to know why your bus was parked behind the church. Elmer Johnson is leading the betting on that you are seriously in the doghouse."

"Damn small town rumor mill," Brantley sighed. Seriousness came into his eyes as he cupped my cheek stroking a calloused thumb softly. "Any regrets baby? I know that...."

"Not a damn one," I growled softly at him narrowing my eyes. A gentle smile tugged at his full lips warming my heart. I wrapped my hand around his wrist returning the smile. "This is so perfectly us B. Plus fairly sure it blows the wedding date pool they have going on down at the hardware store to hell and back. Daddy said Mr. Rogers had some complex algorithm worked out on what date in May it was going to be. But honestly, we have wasted enough time. I'm ready to get on with the rest of our lives. And truthfully, it just didn't feel right planning something big without Mama being there every step of the way. I know Mrs. Dawn, LeCLaire, and Mama Becky would have been more than happy, just not quite the same."

"I know baby girl," he whispered leaning down to kiss me again. That gentle understanding assured me even though we had gone through hell in some ways to be together again, we had made it to the other side. I deepened the kiss feeling the arms holding me squeeze me closer. Felt my feet shuffle back towards the stairs. I raised my hands pushing the cool leather from his shoulders when I was lifted off my feet. Wrapping my legs around his waist I was perfectly fine with the intended destination back up the stairs I had just come down.

"I don't think so," we heard boomed making Brantley growl as a deep blush spread across my cheeks. Twenty-nine years old and I was bright red when I chanced a glance over his shoulder to the two women standing by the front door with hands on their hips. Also, I could see the twinkle in both their eyes at the excitement for both of us. Brantley groaned before unlocking my legs from his waist sitting me down. I smoothed a hand over my braid biting my bottom lip. Mama Becky rolled her eyes at both us shaking a finger. "Save something for the wedding night you two. Son, what happened to not seeing the bride before the wedding."

"Well Becky," LeClaire rasped with a throaty chuckle. "Do you want grand-babies or not?"

"Mama," Brantley sighed rolling his eyes. He bent over grabbing his jacket shrugging back into it. A quick kiss pressed to my lips making me giggle. "Love you. I'll see you later. Gonna have to stay in tough mode today so I don't cry like a baby watching you walk towards me later."

That night as the house grew quiet, I stepped out onto the back deck into the pale glow of the full October moon. Twinkling white lights wrapped around the columns looking like starlight. A soft smile teased my lips thinking of the shared look between Luke and Sadie earlier. No doubt reminding them of their first date. I remember how nervous Luke had been and desperate for help.

A simple reception here at the house after saying our vows. I knew that word we had quietly gotten married was traveling through the town grapevine like wildfire. The rest of the world would find out next week. Daddy had been wiping tears off his cheeks walking me down the aisle. I had barely noticed my eyes firmly fixed on the man at the end of the aisle staring at me like he'd never seen me before. Unable to explain it, I had been comforted in what felt like another arm looped through my other side. Like Mama was there walking with me. I looked down at the bracelet peeking out from the sleeve of my dress. The angel wings and sapphires representing my something old and something blue.

Overwhelming happiness for us had been the only reason Sadie nor Stephanie hadn't killed us for springing a wedding on them. Idle talk one night on the couch had spiraled from there. May had seemed so far away after all the uncertainty between us for so long. Looking down at the diamond band resting under my engagement ring I smiled. All the times we said goodbye I often wondered if this time would be the last. Sure had felt like it a few times.

The idle dreams of that young teenage girl half in love with the senior quarterback felt like a million years ago. Life had turned out nothing like I had thought it would. Though I still was now able to sign my name like I'd envisioned doing my entire freshman year, life's complex obstacles had stepped in over the years. We'd both tried to leave. Tried running for our past. Ran from each other but here we were.

Arms wrapping around my waist as a warm chest melded to my back the soft fabric of Brantley's shirt teasing the open part at the back of my dress. I leaned back into him closing my eyes lacing our hands together. Felt his wedding band click against mine. Wasn't any doubt in my mind this was where I belonged. Always been my home where ever in the world I was, this ultimately had been where I was meant to be.

Epilogue

November 2018

Susanna's POV

I huddled further into my jacket watching the scene before me in the cold Tennessee night. A smiled pulled at my lips thinking of the anxious nervousness on my husband's features a month ago on our one year anniversary. His hands had shaken slightly giving me concern when he handed over a flash drive before pointing at the laptop sitting in my lap. Knew he'd been in the studio so much over the summer I didn't even have to ask if it was something for the upcoming album or not. Brantley bit his lip explaining as I pulled up the file that it was the lead off single for it. That he needed to know what I thought of it.

Paced the living room the three minutes and twenty-three seconds of the song. Tears had immediately sprang forth listening to the words. Absolutely perfect was all I could think wiping at my face. Today had been surreal irony in a lot of ways watching all of this. Heels clicking on the asphalt of the deserted street made my head turn gratefully taking the steaming cup of coffee from the smiling blonde.

"Ah," I sighed with a laugh taking a sip feeling warmer and more awake already. "I have the new mom look big time huh."

"Girl you look absolutely beautiful," Lindsay chuckled shaking her head. We stood there watching the scene in front of us as Brantley took his place in the middle of the street. "How you juggle him, his career, your own, and a little one makes you Superwoman in my eyes. You two were positively nauseating snuggling on the bleachers earlier. Still have that newlywed glow. Makes a person envious."

"I will try to remember that next time he pisses me off," I snickered making her laugh. "Both of your voices on this is amazing."

"But listening to him explain how truthful it is guts me," Lindsay sighed with a soft smile. I nodded my head. "Really does stay in a small town huh?"

"Girl," I laughed throwing my head back laughing. "You have no idea. They pout if we don't give them something to talk about at least once a month. But there is nowhere else either of us would rather be. I remember coming home from France dreading the fact I couldn't hide from him unless he was on tour. Worried about passing him on the road. But it all worked out in the end."

"That it did," I heard chuckled making me look up. Lindsay gave me a wink as my husband approached us. Mason motioned for her. She walked forward taking the guitar she was handed after sitting her coffee down and took her place. Brantley smiled down at me wrapping his arms around me pulling me close. A soft kiss pressed to the crown of my head while I slipped my arms under the leather jacket he was wearing burrowing closer. No matter how hectic life could get for us, this right here always centered me reminding me that there wasn't anything we could get through. "So who won the grandparent lottery today?"

"Last check in," I snickered resting my chin on his chest looking up at him. "Your dad was on baby duty. Daddy had a date. LeClaire passed her turn since Sadie came down to spend a few days with her parents brining all three kids. Though he did mention going by there...."

"The hell he is," Brantley growled flying into action to pull his phone out of his jacket pocket. "I don't want either of those damn Bryan boys near my princess. Not no but hell no."

"Well baby," I teased mercilessly. Green eyes narrowed at me with his phone halfway to his ear. "Guess it would be just desserts in some ways. You know their mama and you....."

"Susanna Grace Gilbert," he snarled shoving his phone back in his jacket. I ducked out of his arms with a yelp backing away as he stalked after me. "You take that shit back right now! Or we will give this entire crew a show!"

"Got to catch me first babe!" I taunted spinning on my heel darting towards his bus. PJ passed me on the way rolling his eyes. "Slow him down for me PJ. My mouth overloaded my ass again."

"Will do Cupcake," PJ chuckled stopping crossing his arms as I got closer to the bus. "Now now Boss.... You know Cupcake."

"Damn right I do," Brantley taunted making me look back over my shoulder with a wide grin. "She's safe for now but it's me she has to ride all the way back to Georgia with. I'll just bide my time wife! Payback is coming!"

"I'm counting on it!" I teased back blowing him a kiss. Brantley rolled his eyes with a smirk before heading back to take his spot to wrap up the video. Loved that man body and soul. Never would get tired of him. I mean, someone had to keep our small town on their toes. Seemed we were the couple to do it.

The End